DRIFT FENCE

ORDNANCE

DRIFT FENCE

Walt Coburn

GUNSMOKE

First published in the UK by Hammond

This hardback edition 2012
by AudioGO Ltd
by arrangement with
Golden West Literary Agency

ISBN 978 1 445 82393 5

British Library Cataloguing in Publication Data available.

Printed ar
MPG Boo

CHAPTER I

ACCORDING to the Montana law of metes and bounds, big Bob Rutledge was measuring off the boundary lines of his cattle ranch which covered one hundred thousand acres of Montana's finest cattle country. Starting from the landmark known as Rutledge Butte, the survey party headed southward towards the badlands of the Missouri River. Bob Rutledge and his foreman, a lanky Texan named Abilene Adams, did the measuring on horseback, employing a fifty-foot reata instead of a surveyor's chain, using landmarks for sights and building rock monuments to fix the boundary lines.

With Bob Rutledge and Ab Adams rode Will Sheppard, the cattleman's attorney. Behind, with the pack outfit, rode Brad Rutledge, Bob's only son, and a giant Negro called 'Chalk.' Their job was to bring along the pack horses and build the rock monuments. Will Sheppard carried a map and a quart bottle of whisky.

'We head south from here,' Bob Rutledge told Sheppard as they consulted the Government map, 'as far as where Beef Creek empties into the Missouri. Then eastward to the mouth of Sand Creek, following the river. North from the mouth of Sand Creek to the Indian Rock, and then due west to Rutledge Butte. We'll measure it off with this rawhide reata I brought from Texas, and in ten years from now I'll own this whole country and make my own laws. I'll be cattle king of Montana, Shep.'

Bob Rutledge was a big square-featured man with tawny hair and moustache now turning grey. He had cold grey-blue eyes and a drawling voice. He towered above the slender, thin-faced Will Sheppard, who was rated the sharpest land attorney and criminal lawyer in the country.

5

Will Sheppard might have been forty or sixty. He looked tubercular and his face was colourless. He had a habit of lifting his left eyebrow and the left corner of his mouth. His eyes were bright blue, shrewd, yet with a humorous twinkle. Never sober, seldom drunk, except after he had finished a difficult case in court, he was known as Bob Rutledge's right-hand bower. They had come together from Texas. Bob Rutledge with his fifty-foot reata and cedar-handled Colts, Will Sheppard with his bottle of whisky and a dingy law library loaded on a pack mule.

'The cattle king of Montana, Shep,' repeated Bob Rutledge, with a sweep of his hard muscled arm. 'I'll own it all.'

'Not for anything in the world, Robert,' said Will Sheppard, his left eyebrow quirking, 'would I dash cold water upon the fire of your dreams, but remember this fact: inside this boundary line is land that you're taking up that may later be contested. I seem to foresee the day, Robert, when you'll need me to keep you from going to prison.'

'I'm taking this land legal. Desert claims, scrip. Every man I got working for me is taking up land. I'll buy it off them. Shep, you talk like a loco sheepherder.'

'I know Montana law, Robert. Government law. State law. And I'm telling you that some day I'll work myself to death to save your thick neck. Drink, Robert?' Will Sheppard was the only man who ever called Bob Rutledge Robert.

Ab Adams, Rutledge's foreman, rode up, dragging the raw-hide reata. Ab was a lean, leathery man with black eyes and greying black hair. He was rated as one of the best cowmen who had ever come up the trail, also as a fast gun fighter. He pulled the back of a gloved hand across his thin-lipped mouth and took the bottle out of Will Sheppard's hand.

Bob Rutledge never went anywhere without Ab Adams or Chalk as a bodyguard, because back in Texas where they came from, Bob Rutledge had been mixed up in one of the bloodiest range wars ever fought. The Rutledge-Banning feud. He had left there with Chalk and Ab Adams and the motherless Brad, then a small boy. Behind them were the fresh graves of the rest of the Rutledge tribe, also more than a few graves filled by the Banning clan. And since word had come out of Texas that Taylor Banning and his brother Tracy were still

6

alive, Bob Rutledge never rode alone, because the Bannings came from a breed that never gives up a grudge.

Now Brad Rutledge rode up, followed by the black giant, Chalk. A tall youth of twenty was Brad Rutledge, with the square blunt features of his father. His eyes were more blue than grey, and he grinned easily. Brad was a good cowhand, and although he lacked the ruthless way of his father, he was never lacking in courage. Brad got forty a month, like the other cowman hands. Bob Rutledge didn't believe in spoiling his son, and he handled Brad with an iron hand.

Brad had never known any affection from his father. He reckoned Bob cared about him, but not like most fathers care for an only son. Chalk had always looked after Brad, and the boy had a lot of real affection for the black giant who loved to laugh and joke and dance jigs. Chalk had looked after Brad since he was a thirteen year old youngster, running away from Texas and a burned home and the newly made grave that held his mother. Chalk worshipped Brad. They had fun together. But Brad had never shared a joke or a laugh with his father or the thin-lipped Ab Adams.

Will Sheppard was different. Shep had acted as both tutor and friend to the boy who saw little of schools as he and his father and Ab Adams and Chalk and Will Sheppard drifted from one place to another. Arizona, New Mexico, Utah and California, where Bob Rutledge had made a huge fortune panning gold on Sutter Creek, then Nevada, where the gambling tables netted more yellow gold, and now to Montana. Always these men and the boy had travelled together, and Shep, through whose strange nature ran the whimsical streak of a dreamer and philosopher, spent long hours teaching Brad such things as Grammar, Latin, Geometry, Shakespeare and how to deal from the bottom of a deck of cards.

As the pack horses started grazing, the white men, the youth and the Negro squatted on their heels in the shade of some big cottonwoods. They ate bread and cold meat and drank from the creek.

7

CHAPTER II

FROM the hogbacked ridge that was covered with scrub pines, two men had been watching the survey party through an old pair of army field glasses. They squatted on their spurred boot-heels and passed the glasses back and forth, and for the most part they were given to silence, except when one or the other of them voiced his thoughts aloud, expecting no reply and getting none.

The two men were Taylor and Tracy Banning. Only a few years marked the difference in their ages and with the sprinkling of grey in their coal-black hair they could have been twins. Cast from the same mould, they had the same tall, lean, long-muscled build, the same straight, coarse black hair and the same high cheekbones and lean jaws. Hawk-beaked, black-eyed, with the same arrogant tilt to their heads. The Banning clan came from Virginia and both brothers were throwbacks to a proud Southern aristocracy, with all the traditions bred in them.

The feud between the Bannings and the Rutledges went back two generations. It had its start when Major Zack Banning serving with the Confederate Cavalry under General Robert E. Lee had refused to surrender. Rather than break his cavalry sabre in defeat he had made the long ride into Texas, locating along the Texas-Mexican border. Still a rebel, wild and hot-blooded, prideful and bitter, he had taken all the rankling poison of defeat with him. The whisky he drank kept the fire of quick resentment burning inside the man.

Captain Sam Rutledge, one of Quantrill's Raiders, was a hard-riding, hard-fighting, swashbuckling adventurer, who lived on danger and whisky, and when Quantrill's Raiders had broken up and disbanded, he had made a running fight of it, until he found the comparative safety of the Texas border,

8

where he had the misfortune to meet up with Major Zack Banning.

Both men were dissimilar by nature. Major Banning was a high-headed aristocrat, while Captain Rutledge was of coarser grain, uncouth, overbearing when drunk. Even sober these men would have clashed. But that night at a Mexican baile both men had been drinking the fiery tequila and mezcal and had fought a gun duel over a Mexican dance-hall girl. Both men were seriously wounded but both recovered from their wounds.

While their ranches bordered, there was the natural barrier of a creek and brush thicket, marking the deadline. Neither man spoke to each other during the years they lived along the border. Each had married and raised a family, and passed the feud along to their children as a heritage.

Then the range war that had been long brewing over the years boiled over and the Bannings and the Rutledges fought on opposite sides. It was a futile war that gained nothing, but the soil of the Lone Star State was spattered and soaked by the blood of brave men and the Banning-Rutledge feud grew more bitter, until Bob Rutledge and his son Brad were the only men left of the Rutledge clan, and Taylor and Tracy Banning the only Bannings left to pick up the feud from their dead.

Eight years . . . ,' Tracy Banning lowered the field glasses, 'or longer. A long time to follow a blood trail, but it looks like this might be the end of it. I still can't figure why Bob Rutledge pulled stakes and quit Texas with his kid between sundown and daybreak. Don't look like a Rutledge would lose his guts overnight.'

Taylor Banning took the glasses and said, 'Don't fool yourself, Bob Rutledge still has plenty guts. He hasn't changed much, neither has Chalk or Abilene Adams. The skinny gent must be the lawyer Will Sheppard, and the kid Brad Rutledge, grown into a man. Sometimes it don't seem right . . . we come into this world naked and bare and when we get old enough, a gun is put into our hand.' Taylor handed the glasses to Tracy.

'That's no way for a Banning to talk, Taylor.'

'Just thinking out loud, that is all. Neither of us has dirtied

9

a gun barrel in over eight years . . . a man kind of gets out of the habit, Tracy.'

'Well don't slow up . . . better keep remembering the oath we took together at our Dad's grave . . . we shook hands on it.'

'I was just thinking of that daughter of mine. . . . The women folks suffer most from feuding. . . . Supposing I get killed?'

'I'll always take care of Georgia if anything happens to you. You should know that.'

'You aren't bullet proof, Tracy.'

Tracy Banning did not offer any reply. When he broke the long silence he had changed the subject.

'All morning Bob Rutledge has been dragging that rope, with Abilene Adams on the other end . . . a fifty-foot rawhide reata as I calculate. They're setting long iron pins with a red rag, and Chalk and Brad are building rock monuments every mile. Following the law of metes and bounds, to mark the boundaries of this free range Rutledge is staking out for himself. Looks like he's claiming half of Montana Territory. But holding on to it is a different story. We just got here in time, Taylor.'

'Yeah. Bob Rutledge tried to do the same thing in Texas, but we ran him out, and we'll run him off the range he's claiming with that rope. He's always been a reata man. . . . Uses that rawhide rope for everything. Surveying the land he's claiming . . . catching other people's cattle. . . . Take that rope away and Bob Rutledge would feel plumb naked.'

'Bob Rutledge will hang by the rope he uses one of these days.' Tracy cut in. 'You mark my word, Taylor.'

'Let's ride on down and let Rutledge know we finally warmed up the cold trail.' Taylor got to his feet and stretched, hitching-up the loaded cartridge belt and holstered six-shooter that sagged around his lean flanks.

'We're outnumbered, Taylor, if you want to make it a showdown.'

'Since when did you start counting the odds, Tracy? We're just letting him and Abilene know we're in the country, claiming range adjoining his and throwing our cattle drive on our BB range.'

10

Tracy shoved the field glasses into the worn case he had strapped to the fork of his saddle and stepped aboard his horse. Taylor Banning led the way down the narrow trail off the scrub-timbered hogback. When they were on level ground Tracy moved his horse alongside that of his brother, so that they made a sinister looking pair as they rode at a running walk towards the Rutledge outfit camped under the giant cottonwoods.

It was one of those sunny Montana days that are meant for pleasure. There was a prairie-dog town on the flat and the prairie dogs barked on a shrill sharp note, scampering back and forth between the high mounds of earth. A long beaked curlew cried . . . a flock of sage hens whirred in flight . . . and somewhere along the creek a meadowlark warbled its liquid noted song.

It might have been some peaceful picnic Bob Rutledge and his pack outfit were enjoying along the creek bank. Only the carbines in the saddle scabbards and the six-shooters worn by Bob Rutledge, Abilene Adams and the giant Chalk gave lie to its peaceful nature. The guns. And the cold, wary eyes of every man there as they watched the two riders cross the prairie-dog town.

Bob Rutledge's harsh rasping voice broke the uneasy silence. 'It's been a long time, a hell of a long time, since I laid eyes on Taylor and Tracy Banning, but I'd know that pair in Hell on a black night.' He walked over to his horse, picked up the bridle reins and mounted. He shook his head as Ab Adams headed for his horse. 'You stay here, Ab. You and Chalk will do more good for a backing where you are.' Bob Rutledge grinned flatly, baring big yellowed teeth, and his eyes were as bleak as a winter sky. 'The Bannings branded me for a rank coward when I quit Texas. I'm riding out alone to meet the two of them. I don't need to tell you what to do, Ab, if they take a notion to gut shoot me.'

'You don't need to tell me anything, Bob.' Abilene Adams said quietly.

As big Bob Rutledge rode out to meet the Banning brothers, Ab Adams kept his hand on his six-gun. Chalk, his eyes showing whitely, sat on his heels, his carbine across his lap. Brad looked at Will Sheppard, and Shep twisted his left eye-

11

brow and the left corner of his mouth. Shep never packed a gun. Niether did Brad. Shep's eyes twinkled brightly, and he uncorked his bottle.

'If they open up the fireworks, Brad, we'll jump in the creek and hide under a cut bank. I've yet to find the use in carrying around a gun and pulling it out and shooting at people. Discretion is the better part of valour, Brad, and when guns go off I run like a rabbit. I might some day be shot in the back, but never will Will Sheppard get shot facing any kind of firearms. Gun-fighting is the pastime of fools, and while I don't deny being a rank coward, no man ever called me a fool.

'Look at Chalk. Nobody ever called him brainy. He'd rather be in a Mexican knife scrap than at a dance. As for the delightful Abilene Adams, past-master of the art of gun fanning, I often wonder what life gives him in the way of pleasure. He never smiles. Never enjoys a drink. If he ever cracked a joke, even a bad joke, he'd choke. And as for singing, he always somehow reminds me of a raven. Poe's Raven-Nevermore. Fits him like a black shroud.

'Now take the Bannings. Great people. Breeding, education, refinement, all that. But gun-toters. Hot-blooded. And some day they'll start in killing one another. But not to-day. Too many on the Rutledge side. A shortage of Banning guns.' Shep lifted his bottle and sipped the raw whisky.

Bob Rutledge rode up within ten feet of the two Bannings. 'You're on my land,' he told them, his voice harsh.

'Hardly, Rutledge. We're on land that you're claiming, but it's not your land.' Tracy Banning's voice was tense. His dark eyes snapped. 'You're marking off land that you're trying to steal. You're not going to get away with it.'

'I reckon you aim to stop me?'

Taylor Banning smiled faintly. Taylor was the cooler headed of the two. 'We aim to do our best to stop you from stealing land that belongs to the Government, Rutledge. News reached Texas that you were going to be the cattle king of Montana. Tracy and I came from Texas to stop you from doing here what you tried to do down there.'

'Whenever you feel lucky,' said Bob Rutledge, sitting with

12

his weight in his left stirrup, his hand on his six-gun, 'open up the jackpot.'

'When we start,' said Tracy Banning, 'we'll run you out of Montana like we ran you out of Texas. We're locating on Antelope Creek. Our land joins yours. We rode here to tell you that we're going to hang that tough hide of yours on the fence. We're ridding Montana of all of you. You can take that message back to that son of yours and your two bodyguards and your crooked shyster.'

Big Bob Rutledge grinned contemptuously. 'And you came all the way from Texas to try a whizzer like that, did you? Well, I'm located here now, and no man is going to run me off. You two snakes better get off my land. If I ever catch you on it again, I'll fill you both full of lead. Git!'

Bob Rutledge sat his horse and watched the Bannings ride back along the trail.

Taylor and Tracy Banning rode along in a heavy silence, each man busy with his own thoughts, his own reactions to their verbal run-in with Bob Rutledge. Both were hot-tempered men, especially Tracy, and they had learned from long experience born of hot-headed bitter words when their viewpoints clashed never to voice an opinion until it had been calmly and carefully thought over. Several times in their younger days they had come to blows that might easily have turned into gunplay, and because they were the last of the Banning clan it behoved them not to quarrel. The bond of blood brotherhood was a stronger tie because of the hot-blooded nature of both men. Their mutual regrets, the aftermath of those violent quarrels, left both brothers too torn up inside.

They topped the scrub-timbered hogback, pulled up and dismounted, both men loosening their saddle cinches to let their sweat-wet winded horses blow.

Taylor Banning fished a short briar pipe and a leather pouch that held a chunk of homemade twist tobacco from his chaps pocket. He whittled the tobacco into the palm of his hand and ground it up with his thumb as he stood there, staring with a brooding scowl, his eyes on the skyline.

Tracy rolled a brown paper cigarette and had it half-

13

smoked by the time the elder brother had his pipe packed and
had touched a match to the tobacco.

Taylor Banning waited until he had filled his lungs with
the strong plug cut tobacco smoke before he broke the silence.

'I'll back up what I said before, Tracy. It wasn't no such
thing as cowardice that drove Bob Rutledge out of Texas.
Until his wife got hit by a stray bullet, the thought of quitting
Texas and whatever part he was taking in the feud never
entered his mind . ; . it was directly after he'd buried his
wife that he took his son and pulled out overnight. It wasn't
because he was scared of being killed. Bob Rutledge is a
coarse-grained, ignorant man, ruthless and cold-blooded. He
might wait till he got the bulge on a man before he drew his
gun and killed, without his conscience bothering him for one
second, but there isn't any yellow streak of fear in his make-
up. With the backing of men like Abilene Adams and Chalk,
he stood slightly better than an even chance of killing the last
two Bannings when he pulled stakes in the night back in
Texas. Figure it out for yourself, Tracy.' Taylor Banning relit his pipe. His grim smile and the flinty look in his black eyes
showed through the tobacco smoke.

'No man ever discounts an enemy, Taylor.' Tracy measured
each word like he was holding his temper under control. A
flat grin slid across his mouth. 'I don't mind admitting to you,
I didn't draw a free breath back yonder as we turned our
backs on that Rutledge outfit till we were out of rifle range.'

'I know. Bob Rutledge and Chalk never shot a man in the
back. But that don't go for Abilene Adams. If he had his way
we'd both be lying dead back at that prairie-dog town.'

'I'm sure glad to hear you aren't softening up to the point
where you love your enemies.'

'You know a damnsight better.'

Tracy Banning pinched out the short butt of his cigarette
and tightened his saddle cinch. He mounted without saying a
word and rode off in silence. Taylor Banning knocked the
last ashes from his pipe on the ground, and rubbed the black
ash into the ground with his boot. Then he re-set his saddle
blanket that had slipped a little on the steep climb, pulled the
cinch tight and rode on, making no move to lift his horse
from the jogtrot that is the gait of a travelling cowboy. And

14

for a few miles Tracy made no move to slow down so that his older brother might overtake him.

It was not until they sighted a cattle drive moving into Antelope Valley that Tracy slowed down enough to let Taylor overtake him. As if he had completely forgotten their near-quarrel, Tracy pointed a long arm towards the big drive of cattle that was now spreading out, spilling into the valley, the thirsty cattle fanned out by the two cowhands who had been riding the point, so that the dry cattle would not pile up along the creek.

'Sure a pretty sight, Taylor. Three thousand head of long-horns and all of them in the Banning iron . . . BB, back to back. . . .' His grin spread to put warmth of pride into his opaque black eyes.

'The end of the long trail,' nodded Taylor Banning. But his eyes were on one of the distant horsebackers who had been riding the point. His puckered black eyes alight, a soft smile on his hard lipped mouth.

'I wanted a son, Tracy.' Taylor Banning mused aloud. 'And I got me a daughter. But Georgia tries to make up for the loss. There isn't a better cowhand anywhere than Georgia Banning.'

'You get no argument out of her Uncle Tracy. Georgia's a good cowhand anywhere you put her . . . fetching up the drags, along the swing or riding the point. . . . Her cousin Joe Slocum's been teaching her how to shoot a gun.'

'The hell he has!' Taylor Banning exploded. 'I'll double a wet rope across that damned spur jingler's back.'

'Simmer down, Taylor,' said Tracy Banning, grinning faintly. 'What you going to do after Joe Slocum marries the girl? You going to live with them so that you can ride close herd on a man's wife?'

Taylor Banning, white-lipped, his black eyes narrowed, fought down the livid anger inside him. The lean weathered hand that gripped his saddle was so tight the knuckles showed bone white.

'Like as not it isn't Joe Slocum's fault. . . . Georgia's trying to be a Banning. . . . She wants to make a hand. . . .'

'Not a gun hand.' Taylor Banning's voice was dry-throated.

'You let the kid run wild after her mother died,' said Tracy

15

Banning. 'You taught her to ride and how to handle horses and cut cattle out of the herd, read brands and earmarks, how to rope and get down on the ground and rassle calves. Georgia growed up a tomboy and you helped her along. Now when Joe Slocum teaches her how to handle a gun, you rile up. Don't put all the blame on cousin Joe . . . he's stuck on the girl.'

'Dry up, Tracy,' Taylor Banning said flatly. 'You never married and had a kid of your own. Me and my daughter understand one another. Georgia never told me she was going to marry Joe Slocum. I hope she never will. Joe Slocum is a killer . . . the same breed as Abilene Adams. . . . Not only that, he can't be trusted too far, even if he is shirt-tail kin to the Bannings and his old man got killed fighting on our side. We've raised him and given him every chance there is, but he's been mixed up in too many killings. Joe Slocum isn't the right kind of a husband for that daughter of mine. I reckon she has sense enough to know it and will do her own picking when the time comes.'

The look in his brother's eyes told Tracy Banning he had gone too far.

'If Georgia was my own kid,' he said quietly, 'I couldn't think more of her. But somehow with the Bannings getting killed off, and Joe Slocum a near cousin and one of the family, it seemed kind of natural for them to some day get married.'

'Georgia will never marry him, if I can prevent it.'

'Have it your own way, Taylor. But it looks like now is a good time for the Bannings to stick together.'

Their eyes met and held and then softened and the same grin spread across the faces of Taylor and Tracy Banning. They rode along now, side by side. It was Taylor who spoke first.

'You notice one thing, Tracy?' Taylor asked. 'Young Brad Rutledge don't pack a gun.'

'Yeah' was all Tracy said.

They rode on in silence, watching the spread-out cattle water and graze. The chuck wagon and bed wagon and remuda were already camped up the creek above the cattle.

It looked like a cattleman's paradise.

Joe Slocum and Georgia Banning had stopped their horses

16

on the creek bank under the giant cottonwoods. The high willow thicket along the creek hid them from sight. The other BB cowhands had turned loose the herd and were headed for camp.

As the two Banning brothers rode through the scattered cattle they heard the sound of Joe Slocum's voice, half-bantering, half-annoyed, and Georgia's soft drawl answering.

'How long you going to put a man off, anyhow?' Joe Slocum was saying.

'I'm not putting you off, Joe . . . you're just taking too much for granted. If ever I decide to marry you, I'll let you know. Until then, hands off.' Georgia softened her reprimand with a soft laugh.

'Men have a name for girls like you, that tease a man along and when he reaches out they freeze-up. It ain't no nice name. I reckon you must have heard it around cow camps!'

Taylor and Tracy Banning rounded a bend in the creek, just in time to see Joe Slocum crowd his horse against the girl's, and reach one long arm around her waist. Georgia swung her loaded rawhide quirt across his eyes. The man recoiled.

'You damned little hellcat.'

Taylor Banning spurred his horse to a run, coming up from behind. Before Joe Slocum could twist around in his saddle Taylor Banning had him by the throat, jerking him backwards out of his saddle and going to the ground with him as he fell. Straddle of the younger man, his thumbs bit deep into Joe Slocum's windpipe. Joe Slocum was young, well-built, tough in any kind of a rough and tumble fight, but the older man had the advantage from the start. He never let go until Slocum's face purpled and his jaw sagged. Then Tracy Banning was pulling Taylor off, and had all he could do to hold him after he got him pulled free. Taylor Banning's face was livid, his black eyes murderous.

Georgia Banning, dressed in chaps and denim jacket and a shapeless hat pulled down across her head, looked on, her face pale under the powdering of dust. The freckles across her nose stood out blackly and her dark brown eyes were wide with horror.

Joe Slocum's black hair was matted with sweat and dirt.

17

He moaned as he rolled clear, his hands at his bruised throat. He got up on to his hands and knees and then on to his feet, the congested colour leaving his face pale. His eyes narrowed to bloodshot pale grey slivers. His right hand was moving slowly towards the ivory-handled six-shooter when Tracy Banning spoke, his voice flat-toned.'

'Fork your horse, Joe, and ride off somewheres till Taylor cools off.'

'If ever you lay a hand on my daughter again, you damned inbred whelp, I'll kill you.' Taylor warned him.

'Quit it!' Georgia Banning's voice was brittle as smashed glass. 'It's all my fault. Don't blame Cousin Joe, Papa. Will you . . . is it too much to ask . . . too late for you all to shake hands. Please, Papa . . . Joe. . . . Do something, Uncle Tracy!'

CHAPTER III

BOB RUTLEDGE had built himself a big log house with every convenience his money could buy. There were several bedrooms, each with a bath, and a long hallway. The place had hardwood floors, natural log walls, a huge rock fireplace, and pictures made by Montana's great artist, Charlie Russell, hung from the walls. On the floor were the Indian tanned hides of silvertip grizzlies. In front of the big fireplace was an Indian tanned cowhide that wore Bob Rutledge's Block R brand.

When the survey party got home from the trip of measuring off the domain of the big cowman, Bob Rutledge drove a wooden peg into the log wall above the fireplace. On the wooden peg he hung the rawhide reata. Ab Adams, Brad and Will Sheppard looked on. Chalk brought in a whisky decanter made of cut glass, and glasses of the same pattern. The whisky was twenty years old.

'As old as Brad,' said Bob Rutledge as he filled the glasses. Will Sheppard looked at the rawhide reata hanging on the peg above the rock fireplace. He did not seem to notice the drink at his elbow. Bob Rutledge poured Brad a drink. Ab Adams sat in his rawhide-seated chair, twisting his filled glass in his hand. Chalk stood behind Brad's chair, his black face unsmiling, a worried look in his eyes. Never before had Bob Rutledge ever given his son a drink.

Standing before the fireplace on widespread legs, he lifted his glass. 'You'll drink to the Block R, gents,' he said.

Will Sheppard got to his feet, slowly. He took the filled glass from Brad's hand and tossed it into the fire. Then, his left eyebrow twisted upward, he smiled crookedly at Bob Rutledge. 'I'll do Brad's share of drinking, Robert!'

Bob Rutledge tensed. His cold eyes were narrowed now. Brad was on his feet, white-lipped, fists clenched, as his father took a step towards Will Sheppard.

'Shep's right,' said Brad in a husky voice. 'I'm not drinking. Not now, or ever. You can't make me!'

Ab Adams moved a little in his chair. Bob Rutledge shifted his hard-eyed glare to his son. Brad stood firm on his feet, steady eyed, between Will Sheppard and his father.

'I'm boss here,' growled Bob Rutledge. 'I'll skin alive the man that tries to cross me.'

'Robert,' said Will Sheppard, stepping around Brad, 'nobody is hurting Brad. Take it out on me if you like, but leave Brad alone. If you don't, you'll regret it. I'd advise you to sit down.'

Bob Rutledge looked from Will Sheppard to the white-lipped Brad, then at Chalk and Ab Adams.

Ab Adams lifted his glass. 'Here's how,' he said, and tossed off his drink. 'If I was you, Bob, I'd sit down. Shep's right. If Brad don't want to drink, don't crowd him.'

Chalk's hand came away from the bowie knife he always carried. He grinned widely.

'Robert,' said Will Sheppard, 'you're out-voted. Ab, my congratulations. From that barren heart of yours there sprouts the small but unmistakable branch of human understanding. A quality so long dormant that it . . .'

'Who asked you to make a speech?' cut in Ab Adams, reaching for the decanter.

19

Will Sheppard grinned faintly, 'Robert,' he said. 'Your health. And may that rawhide reata never hang you.'

'Meaning,' said Bob Rutledge, 'just what, Shep?'

'Meaning, Robert, that better and worse men than you have stretched rope. Rawhide rope. As I told you before, some day you'll need me badly to keep you from hanging. But I'd go further for you than any man I know save Brad Rutledge. Robert, I'd enjoy the mate to this libation I've just surrounded and conquered.

'And now, gentlemen, a toast to the future cattle king of Montana. To the health, the success and the eternal prosperity of a man who is, in spite of himself, my friend. The bravest man I have ever known, and the most ruthless enemy that ever a man could wish for. Here's howdy, Robert.'

A strange bond of friendship tied together Bob Rutledge and Will Sheppard. No man save the two knew its beginning, its strength.

When they had emptied their glasses, Bob Rutledge held out his hand. Behind his grin, behind the cold light in his eyes, was something that only Will Sheppard could understand.

'Shake, Shep.'

And later that evening Bob Rutledge and Will Sheppard sat alone in the same room. They sat talking until dawn. In the end Bob Rutledge again put out his hairy paw.

'You'll take care of Brad in case they get me?'

'You don't need to ask that, Robert. I can only hope that, when they get you, they won't get Brad.'

'Or you, Shep.'

'Or me, Robert.'

CHAPTER IV

It had rained for three days and nights. The creeks were bank-full. Brad Rutledge, leading circle, had dropped his

cowboys off in pairs to gather the cattle out of the rough badlands. Slickers were dripping. The red and yellow and grey
mud was balling the feet of the horses. The sky was the
colour of lead. Brad, riding alone, swung up Antelope Creek
to finish the circle, and then cut across to where the cattle
would be gathered.

Antelope Creek was a mud-colored, foam-spotted torrent
there where the cottonwoods grew and the grass was stirrup-
high. The rain beat into Brad's face, and he rode hunched over
the saddle horn, hat pulled low. His horse knew the way, and
he let the big bay gelding travel on a slack rein.

Then, out of the grey mist and rain, out of the silence,
came the terrified scream of a woman.

Brad jerked erect. Fifty yards upstream he saw a horse in
the creek. The horse was pawing madly at the muddy water.
Then he caught a glimpse of a girl's head below the horse.
Brad knew how horses acted in swimming water. He knew
that the fear-stricken animal would paw down the girl. Those
shod hoofs, in their maddened effort to find foothold, would
beat down the girl, who had struck out for the bank of the
creek, trying to fight the swirling current.

Brad jerked his rope free and spurred his big bay into the
creek. The horse was a good water-horse and Brad knew
how to handle it in swimming water. They were between the
girl and her horse now. Brad threw her the rope. She clutched
at it, missed. He called out to her and made another throw.
This time she caught it.

'Hang on!' called Brad. 'I'm giving you a tow. Water wet?'
he asked, and his grin took some of the panic out of her heart,
for she managed a faint reply.

'It's damp, cowboy!'

'Hang on to that rope, lady. Let my horse pull you ashore.'
He had tied his rope hard and fast to the saddle horn when
he saw the girl's horse headed for them.

Brad quit his horse. He manœuvred in behind the girl's
horse, then alongside, slapping water into the face of the
swimming animal. Out of the corner of his eye he saw his
big bay drag the girl ashore. He saw her try to stand on her
feet, then go down in a wilted heap. A few moments later he
had fought her horse ashore and sloshed through the mud

21

to where she lay. He was chilled to the bone, and his lungs were half-full of water, which he coughed up. Down across his face· was a ragged cut where a shod hoof had brazed his head.

The girl's face was blue and pinched with cold. She looked dead, but her pulse was beating slowly. Brad had some dry matches in a tobacco can. Building a fire in the rain was no easy job, but he managed to get a good fire going, then he made clumsy first-aid efforts to revive the girl.

It was some fifteen minutes before his efforts were rewarded. Then he remembered the bottle of whisky in his saddle pocket that belonged to Shep. He forced some of it down the girl's throat, almost choking her. She fought him off blindly, then opened her eyes.

'Take it easy, lady. I was just trying to get a drink down you.' He handed her the bottle. 'Take a swallow. You looked peaked.'

'Thanks, but I don't drink the stuff.'

'Then I'll have to pour it down you,' said Brad. 'Because it's medicine and you need it. I just pumped a gallon of creek water out of you. I don't drink it either, but I'm going to take a swallow to take the chill away.'

Brad put more wood on the fire, and they sat on a cottonwood log beside the warming blaze. The colour was coming back into the girl's face, and she smiled a little. Brad saw that she had hazel eyes and a grim little mouth and copper coloured hair. He bet himself that she was mighty pretty, thawed and dried out. She was dressed in cowboy clothes, and looked like a slim boy. They poured the water out of their boots, and Brad piled more wood on the fire. It had begun to clear up. The rain was a thin mist now. The fire was warming them.

'Need another drink of that whisky, lady?'

'Not me, cowboy. Help yourself.'

Brad grinned. 'Me neither. Makes a man feel warm and kinda dizzy. That's the first time I ever tackled it.'

'But you had a bottle along?'

'Shep's. I pack it for him.'

'And just who is Shep? A sheepherder?'

22

'Shep's no sheepherder. He's about the smartest man in the world, bar none.'

Just then three men rode up out of the rain.

'Here comes company,' Brad said. 'And I'm on the wrong side of Antelope Creek.'

One of the riders was Tracy Banning. The other two rode horses wearing the BB brand.

The girl and Brad were on their feet now. The girl smiled at Tracy Banning.

'Hello, Uncle Tracy. Get down and enjoy the fire. How's this for duck weather?'

'Duck season,' said Tracy Banning, stepping down off his horse and unbuttoning his slicker, 'don't open for a week or two. But it's always open season for coyotes. What are you doing on this side of the boundary, young Rutledge?'

Tracy Banning's face was a dark, sinister mask. His hand was on his gun. The other men sat their horses.

Brad's jaws tightened. Never had he more resembled his father than now when he faced Tracy Banning.

'I never meant to cross your boundary, Banning,' he said slowly. 'Willingly, I wouldn't set foot on your land for all the cattle in Montana. I don't pack a gun. If you were anywhere near my age and size, I'd ask you to take off your gun and fight like a man. Begging the lady's pardon, I reckon she's a Banning. I'm forking my horse, mister. I'm busting that creek and going back on to Rutledge range, unless you're the breed of polecat that shoots men in the back.'

Blood wet Brad's injured face. He was water-soaked, half-chilled, but his eyes were as hard as blue ice, and his grin was the grin of big Bob Rutledge. He stepped up on the big bay horse, and the next moment he and the horse were in the middle of the swollen creek.

If Brad had looked back he would have seen the girl standing by the fire, hot tears blinding her eyes. She was trying to call out to him, but her voice was choked.

Tracy Banning, his gun in his hand, stood there in the thin drizzle. The cowboys with him watched as Brad Rutledge and his bay horse fought the terrific muddy current that carried them downstream like so much driftwood. Man and horse went under and were lost to sight for a moment. Then they showed again, black spots on the muddy, foam-flecked water. A bend in the creek hid them.

'Save him!' sobbed the girl.

'Save a Rutledge?' said Tracy Banning. 'I reckon not. Let the coyote drown.'

Two hundred yards downstream, Brad and the big bay came ashore. Both waterlogged, but both with the same game heart, they rode up a cut coulee and were lost in the rolling hills.

An hour later Brad rode into camp. He unsaddled and took care of his horse, then went to the mess tent. Only the cook was at camp. Brad drank some hot coffee and saddled the horse Ab Adams had left tied to the rear wheel of the bed wagon. The rest of the outfit had eaten their dinner, changed horses, and gone out to work the cattle brought in on the morning circle. Blue sky was showing through the grey clouds. Brad had bandaged his face. As he rode towards the hold-up grounds, he kept thinking of the hazel-eyed girl who had called Tracy Banning her uncle.

'Get lost?' asked Ab Adams when Brad showed up where they were working the cattle. His tone of voice was like the sting of acid.

'If I was,' said Brad, his voice a little sullen, 'I wouldn't admit it.'

'You're two hours late,' said Ab Adams. 'Get in there and start cutting out those cows and calves. We've got a big branding to do. Some day you'll learn this cattle business, maybe. Been asleep in some coulee, I reckon.'

Brad's jaws tightened. 'Don't talk to me like that, Ab. Not ever again. I got my fill of abuse. Keep that in mind.' Brad rode off into the hold-up.

Ab Adams looked after Brad, a faint smile on his lipless mouth. It was a smile that might have meant almost anything.

CHAPTER V

RANGE gossip spreads like a prairie fire driven by a wind. In a week the cow country knew that Brad Rutledge had saved the life of Georgia Banning, daughter of Taylor Banning. By the time that word got to Bob Rutledge, the tale had grown, as such tales grow, until the story went so far as to claim that Brad and Georgia were getting ready to run off and get married.

When the Block R outfit brought in their herd for the first shipment, Bob Rutledge was on the prod. When the last carload of steers were loaded, Bob called Brad off to one side of the empty corrals. Brad had been working without sleep for twenty-four hours. He was sweaty and dusty, and his eyes were red-rimmed.

'What's all this about you and the Banning girl?' growled Bob Rutledge in a surly voice.

Brad's gloved hand instinctively passed across the scar on his jaw that was partly hidden by sweat-streaked dust.

'What do you mean, Dad?' Brad asked, dust clogging his throat, so that he talked in a husky whisper.

'I hear you and Taylor Banning's daughter are going to run off and get married. I'd rather see you dead.'

Brad said, 'I don't know where you got the notion, but you got it all wrong.' Brad's eyes did not waver as he looked at his father.

'You wouldn't turn out to be a sneaking liar, would you?'

'No.' Brad's voice hardened a little: 'Is that all you want of me?'

'Not all. You're getting almighty independent all of a sudden. Shep and Chalk have spoiled you. From now on, Ab Adams will give you orders, and you'll take them or I'll bust your neck. Ab's ramrodding this outfit. You'll do what he tells you. Where there's smoke there's fire, and everybody in the

25

country is saying that my son is stuck on a Banning girl.'

'Who was it told you?' asked Brad, breathing hard, his tongue moistening cracked lips.

'Ab told me how you fished that Banning brat out of the creek, then let Tracy Banning run you off their range. A fine son you are. From now on you pack a gun, and if I ever catch you mingling with that Banning tribe, I'll horsewhip you.'

Bob Rutledge whirled his horse and rode off towards town. Brad, white-lipped and shaking inside, watched his father ride away. Then he rode over to where Ab Adams was tallying up the cattle shipped.

'Pull out for camp,' said Ab Adams in his flat-toned voice. 'Throw the remuda in the big pasture, and tell the horse wrangler he can come to town. You stay at camp and take care of things. Drag it.'

On his way to camp, Brad kept thinking over his father's bitter accusations. After all, he couldn't blame his father. For years the Bannings and the Rutledges had hated. That hatred had cost the lives of brave men on both sides. Even Brad's mother, hit by a wild bullet, had died down there in Texas. Chalk had told Brad that when Brad's mother had died, there in the cabin on the Rutledge ranch in Texas, something inside of Bob Rutledge must have died with her.

It was Bob Rutledge's promise to his dying wife, not fear of the Bannings, that had driven Bob Rutledge out of Texas. He was the breed of man who gives all his love to but one woman. And when she asked him to take Brad and quit Texas and the feuding, he had given her his word, and had kept it, though moving out as he did had branded him as a coward.

Perhaps that was why Bob Rutledge never gave Brad the love a father should give his son. Perhaps deep in his heart he blamed the boy for the brand of coward that the Bannings had stamped on his tough hide when he quit Texas with Ab Adams and Chalk. Bob Rutledge had given his promise and kept it.

In New Mexico they had got into some sort of cattle-rustling scrape. Chalk had taken the rap for them and had spent some time in the New Mexico penitentiary before Bob

Rutledge managed to get him pardoned. It was in the pen Chalk had met Will Sheppard, and when he got his pardon Chalk had waited on the outside for Will Sheppard, who had made his escape over the wall. From then on Shep had been one of them and acted as legal adviser to Bob Rutledge.

Brad wondered what Shep would say about the girl. Would he side in with Bob Rutledge? Or would he tell Brad to pull stakes and lead his own life, and, if possible, get Georgia Banning to run off with him.

Brad rode on to camp and caught a fresh horse, which he staked out. He told the half-breed horse wrangler to shove the remuda in the pasture and go to town, and take the cook with him.

When the horse jingler and the cook had gone, Brad was alone in camp. It seemed lonesome with no cowboys around, the empty bed tent and mess tent, the mess wagon gone.

It was a little past noon. Brad took a swim in the shallow creek and shaved. He put on clean clothes. Then he sat on the creek bank and played mumble-the-peg, left hand against the right. The sun was warm. Big, fleecy clouds changed shape in the blue sky, and Brad, tiring of his lone game, lay flat on his back and conjured odd images out of the clouds. Then sleep came. It was the heavy sleep of a tired cowboy. He came awake with a start, sitting bolt upright. He found himself blinking at Georgia Banning.

'I took the wrong trail, and here I am,' she said, getting down from her horse.

Brad got to his feet. He felt foolish, ill at ease, but only for a moment. He took the hand she held out to him, then dropped it.

'I'm afraid we've stirred up a lot of trouble,' she said. 'I caused it. You saved my life, Brad Rutledge, and I'll never forget it. I'll always be grateful.'

'I'd be plumb tickled to do it over again, ma'am.'

'And I'd be plumb tickled to have you do it, Brad. My name is Georgia. Can't we be friends in spite of all this talk of range war and gun-fighting?'

'That's my idea, Georgia. Like Shep says, gun-toting is done by fools. I wish you could know Shep. I reckon I know what the Bannings call Will Sheppard, but way down deep inside

27

him he's the greatest man I ever met. He's kind inside. He understands things that no other man I ever met could understand. He don't like guns and gun-fighting. Some day he's going to tell me why. I bet it will be a story that'll bear listening to.'

'I'd like to hear it,' said the girl, as they sat on the creek bank. 'From what you say, I know I'd like your Shep.'

'I bet you would,' said Brad. 'Ever play mumbly-peg?'

'Born and brought up on a cow ranch, and you ask me that,' she laughed. 'Bet I beat you, Brad, with your own knife.'

Brad lost the first game and had to pull the small wooden peg from the ground with his teeth. Then Georgia lost. She was rooting at the peg, her small nose in the dirt, when a man on horseback topped the hill above the camp.

Georgia's face was flushed, her hazel eyes dancing, as she held the peg between her white teeth. To Brad Rutledge she was the most beautiful girl in all the world. Then she saw the approaching rider and wrinkled her dirt-smeared nose in a grimace. She handed the wooden peg to Brad, who grinned and put it in his shirt pocket.

Brad knew that something was wrong to bring the cowboy to camp. He pulled up his sweatmarked horse and was a little excited.

'Better get to town, Brad,' he said briefly. 'Bob Rutledge and Taylor Banning shot it out on the street in town. They're both bad hurt.'

CHAPTER VI

THE little cow-town of Alkali had no hospital, though it supported seven saloons. The wounded men were taken to the hotel. Doctors were due to arrive from Great Falls and Helena on the next train. Meanwhile, in their hotel rooms, Bob Rutledge and Taylor Banning lay on blood-soaked mattresses and sheets in opposite rooms just across the hall.

'Ab,' growled Bob Rutledge, 'gimme my gun. I'll crawl to finish Taylor Banning. Gimme my gun, I tell you.'

But Chalk's giant black hands held Bob Rutledge in bed. 'Ah reckon you got him, boss. You dropped him like as if he was a beef,' said Chalk.

'Where's Ab?'

'Just outside the door, boss, standing guard. Ain't no Banning gents getting past Ab or ol' Chalk.'

'Where's Shep? Why ain't he here?'

'Mistah Shep, he say to tell you-all he's handling law business for you. Important law business. Boss, that was a shore enough lead swappin'. Just out and at 'em. No cuss words, no hollerin', no fuss. Just out with them hawg laigs and she comes the Fourth of July. Just like shootin' dice. And out of line stands me and Ab, covering Tracy Banning so he ain't got a rabbit's chance to cut in. The most politest gun fight I ever had the pleasure to look at. Mistah Shep say for you to swaller down this liquidation he left. He says if the lead slugs ain't ruined you, you'll plumb enjoy this twenty-year-old rye.'

Chalk poured the rye down Bob Rutledge's throat. He had been shot three times, once through the chest, once through the shoulder, and the third shot had gone through his thigh without hitting the bone.

The town doctor was dividing his time between the two patients.

Across the hall, Taylor Banning lay on his back, his eyes shut. The doctor had given him something to put him to sleep, then had dug out two bullets from his side and one from his leg. Tracy Banning sat on a chair in the corner of the room, a sawed-off shotgun across his lap, a six-gun and carbine on the table beside him. Outside the door, two heavily armed cowboys stood guard. They glared at the poker-faced Ab Adams, who had a six-gun in each hand as he leaned against the door of Bob Rutledge's room.

The little town of Alkali was boiling with excitement. Men, all packing guns, stood in groups on the plank sidewalks or leaned against the bars in saloons. The town was filled with cowpunchers who worked for Bob Rutledge. And now, at sun-

29

down, cowboys from the Banning outfit were riding in from their round-up camp, ten miles out of town.

The Mercantile had closed and barred its doors. One or two saloons, also, had shut their doors. There was a tenseness in the air. Men talked in low tones. They stayed in groups. Cold, hard eyes watched the Banning cowboys as they rode down the dusty street, hats slanted, six-guns handy. Spurs dragged along the broad plank sidewalks. Block R cowboys glared sullenly at the punchers from the BB wagon. The saloon men were uneasy. The tinhorns were wary and inwardly cursing the luck that was spoiling their games, because the cowboys from both outfits were thinking of other things besides cards and whisky and the dance-halls.

'Every man keep cold sober,' Ab Adams sent out word to his outfit. 'And stay out of the games. I want you on your feet if I need you. Keep your horses saddled and tied to the hitch racks handy, because it looks like a big night.'

The Banning men had much the same orders. Gradually the town was separated into two factions. On the north side of the street the Block R cowboys held forth. The cowboys from the BB outfit walked up and down the south side, their spurs let out to the 'town hole' and fight in their eyes. Each faction was waiting for orders from headquarters. It would take but some trivial thing now to open up a war, there on the street.

At the sheriff's office was a group of armed men. The grizzled old sheriff, a one-time Ranger, chewed on a cold cigar as he listened to what Will Sheppard was saying.

Sheppard's cheeks were drawn and white, save for the telltale red spots on his cheekbones. Once he coughed and the handkerchief that came away from his mouth was stained red.

'Like sitting on a keg of giant powder, sheriff, with the fuse sputtering.' Sheppard quirked his left eyebrow and smiled. 'The village vet says that either or both of them may die before morning. If that happens, this street is going to look like a. Chicago slaughterhouse. No chance of disarming those men on the street?'

'It would be a big job for a small army, but I'm going to try it,' the sheriff said. 'I'll divide my men, and we'll go down both sides of the street. I'll take the Banning side. I'm deputising you to take care of the Rutledge crowd. They know you,

30

and they might give in. Ab Adams is the right man for the job you'll have.'

'Ab Adams won't leave Bob Rutledge, sheriff. Besides, he wouldn't take the job you've so kindly wished on me. It was Ab's idea that the Block R cowboys buy up all the ammunition at the Mercantile. Ab is not what you might call a pacifist. Well, let's get started. I'll do my best.'

'Here's a shotgun, Sheppard. And a six-gun.'

'I might hurt myself with them, thanks. I'll manage without the heavy artillery. And now let's. . . . Hold everything!'

Shep pointed to a couple of riders coming along the street, side by side. Coming at a long lope were Brad Rutledge and Georgia Banning. Riding straight down the street, between the groups of staring, armed cowboys, they rode the gauntlet.

Cowpunchers on both sides of the street began to shift uneasily. Here and there a grin showed as they watched Brad and Georgia swing off their horses and go together into the hotel.

'And now,' said Will Sheppard, 'is where we get in our good work, sheriff. Follow my lead.'

Shep walked up the middle of the street, tall, nonchalant, dressed in a fastidious, almost foppish garb of grey and white and crimson. Grey suit, white shirt and crimson tie. He wore a red carnation in his buttonhole, powdered a bit now by the dust left hanging in the air from the hoofs of the horses ridden by Brad and Georgia. Behind him came the sheriff and a dozen deputies.

Shep stopped in the middle of the street. He made a gesture for silence, and a hush fell over the crowd that gathered from both sides of the street.

'Gentlemen,' said Shep. 'Bob Rutledge and Taylor Banning fought a duel a few hours ago. They fought because of that charming young lady and that young cowboy who just rode into town. The young lady and the young cowboy rode stirrup to stirrup. They seemed to be anything but unfriendly. Men, it looks like a horse on us. We've money in our pockets, and on both sides of the street we behold palaces of entertainment. Check your guns with the sheriff, boys, and the drinks are on me. Who's with me?'

31

'We all are,' roared a cowboy, and the thunderous chorus took it up.

Bob Rutledge stared hard at his son, standing by his bedside. 'Pull up a chair and sit down,' he said. 'You, Chalk, go hunt up Shep and tell him to get here or he'll be too late. What's all that shouting down the street?'

Ab Adams came in just in time to hear the question. His lean face was twisted in a sardonic grin.

'Shep made a speech, right after Brad and Georgia Banning rode down the street together. Now our cowboys and the BB men are all the same as brothers. They've buried the hatchet.'

'With me dying here?' snarled Bob Rutledge. 'Brad, what about you riding into town with the Banning girl? What's the meaning of it, anyhow?'

'We came to town together when we got the news about the gun duel, that's all.'

Bob Rutledge sat up in bed, opening his bandaged wound in the effort. His square face was drawn into hard, bitter lines. His bloodshot eyes were narrowed, blue-grey slits, like knife blades lying in blood. From under his pillow he took his six-gun. There were four notches on the cedar butt of the gun.

'Each notch on his gun tallies a dead Banning,' he said in a hard, gritty voice that had lost its Texas drawl. 'The old sawbones tells me I'm likely to die. He tells me that Taylor Banning hasn't got much chance to live. If he dies, there'll still be Tracy Banning. If I die, there'll be you, Brad. This gun will belong to you. Take it and kill Tracy Banning where you find him. Swear it. Stand on your feet and swear it. Swear it, I tell you!'

'I never packed a gun,' replied Brad, trying to keep his voice steady. 'I'm not killing any man.'

Chalk had gone to fetch Shep. Ab Adams, Brad and his father were alone in the room.

'The Bannings killed your own mother,' Bob Rutledge told Brad, 'I'm dying from Banning lead. And you aren't man enough to play the chips I'm leaving you when I shove back my chair. You're throwing in with the Bannings. Quitting your own father for a Banning woman. What kind of a whelp are you, anyhow? I got a mind to kill you where you stand. Ab, throw him out.'

32

Brad faced Ab Adams. 'Just a second, Ab. I got a word or two to say to my father. Stand away from me.' Brad's voice was harsh, rasping, thick with emotion. He looked at his father, at the big, cedar-handled gun with its grim, notched tally of dead men.

'I'll stick with you, Dad. Always. But I'm not killing anybody. I'm not a killer. I won't go back to the ranch. Not till you send for me. You're hurt bad. I'll be where Chalk and Shep can find me. But don't send Ab Adams after me, ever.'

Brad turned away from the bed where his father sat propped against the pillows. He faced Ab Adams, who stood there, his hand on his gun.

'Better stand to one side,' said Brad, his fists knotted, 'or I'll give you what I've always wanted to give you. Stand aside, or I'll shove that gun down your throat.'

'No man can talk to Ab Adams like that.' His long-barrelled gun slid from its tied-down holster.

'Put it up!' Bob Rutledge said flatly. The gun in his hand made an ominous click as he thumbed back the hammer.

Abilene Adams turned slowly, the gun still in his hand. Bob Rutledge's gun was cocked and pointed at Ab's lean belly. For a long moment their eyes met and held, then Ab shoved his gun slowly back into its holster.

Abilene Adams still blocked the doorway. Brad took one swift step forward. His fist crashed into the killer's jaw and as he reeled backwards, off balance, Brad closed in, following it up with short, straight arm punches. Ab Adams' head rocked back and forth under the impact. He reeled backwards into the hallway, Brad crowding him close.

The door of Taylor Banning's room stood open. The wounded man lay in bed, propped up by pillows and a gun in his hand. Tracy still sat in the chair in the corner, a sawed-off shotgun across his knees. Both brothers could see all that went on in the hallway. Georgia Banning, sitting on the far side of the bed, was also watching, her face a little white.

Brad hammered Ab Adams against the wall. Adams tried to cover his battered face with his forearms and elbows and Brad kept trying to knock his guard down. Then he sunk his fist in under Adams' short ribs. As Ab doubled up, his wind half-knocked out, he clawed for his gun.

33

Then Brad tore into him. Ab's long legs buckled and he went down slowly, his head lobbing sideways, his long back sliding down against the wall. He was out like a light, the gun part way out of the holster, still gripped in his hand.

Brad stood over the man, breathing hard through his nose, the light of battle still in his eyes.

Ab Adams looked for all the world like some beat-up drunk, sitting propped against the wall, his long legs doubled under him, his head sagged in a drunken stupor, his eyes slowly opening to thin slivers. Brad stood back, waiting for him to come alive, watching to see if he would try to use the half-drawn gun in his hand. Ab had lost his hat and his iron-gray hair lay dank across his forehead, to partly screen his slitted eyes.

Brad's lips bared to show his teeth. 'Quit playing possum, Ab. Let go of your gun or use it, or I'll kick your face in.'

Ab Adams lifted his head slowly. His face was a smear of blood and his narrowed eyes looked murderous. His long fingers spread away from the butt of his six-shooter and he used the heel of his hand to slide the gun back into its holster. He licked the blood from his battered lips and spat it out on the worn hall carpet. He opened his mouth as if he was about to say something and then his eyes slid away from Brad's, swivelling sideways, and now he was staring slit-eyed at the giant Negro Chalk, who had come up the stairway and stood at the end of the hallway, his hand on his gun.

Chalk's big rowelled Mexican spurs chimed with each slow step as he came down the hallway. 'Get up on your legs,' he told Ab. 'Go back into Mistah Bob's room and wash the blood off.' He watched Ab get up and walk into the room, closing the door behind him.

'Mistah Will wants to see you,' Chalk told Brad. 'Downstairs.'

For the first time Brad looked across the hall into the Banning room. He was looking into the hazel eyes of Georgia Banning. A slow flush crept into her tense white face and she gave Brad a flat, fleeting smile.

Brad turned and walked downstairs to where Will Sheppard stood leaning idly against the large post of the stair banister. Like he was a self-appointed unarmed guard against the heavily armed cowhands of both outfits who milled in and out between the hotel lobby and the adjoining bar. Will Sheppard's twisted smile lifted a sardonic eyebrow as Brad licked his skinned knuckles. 'You killed Abiline?' he asked.

'No. Just taught him a lesson he'll remember.'

'Abilene won't forget.' Will Sheppard looked worried. 'You should have heeded my warning to stay clear of Abilene Adams. Your second mistake was not killing him.'

'I know, Shep. Things happened upstairs. I quarrelled with my father. Right when he needs me most. He disowned me. Told Ab to throw me out of his sick room. It takes quite a mighty brave man to quarrel with his dying father.' Brad's self-accusation was bitter.

'You go down to my cabin, Brad. Wait there till I come. And quit feeling sorry about anything. I'll patch things up.' Will Sheppard smiled. 'Chalk has been begging for a long time to gut shoot the genial Abilene. I might give him permission.'

'No. I'll do my own fighting, Shep.'

'My mistake, Brad. Now trot down to my cabin. I'll be there as soon and quick as I can make it.'

Will Sheppard walked Brad to the door and opened it and bowed him out. 'Wait for me,' he said and closed the door.

Will Sheppard almost collided with Georgia Banning at the head of the stairs. He was coming up the steps with lowered head. And Georgia's eyes were half-blinded by unshed tears. He bowed stiffly from the waist, removing his hat. Then he spoke in a low tone.

'Permit me the honour of introducing myself to a lady of courage. I am Will Sheppard, known to my closer acquaintances as "Shep." My domicile and office is a log cabin on the outskirts of town, conveniently adjacent to the local bastille. You will find Brad Rutledge waiting there for you. Avoid the main street and nobody will see you in the dim twilight.'

Will Sheppard bowed around the girl and was gone down the hall before she could think of anything to say.

Shep opened the door of Bob Rutledge's room and walked in under the three guns and closed the door behind him.

Georgia Banning stood there for a long moment, her hand

35

gripping the banister. Then she blinked the tears away from her eyes and went out, her mouth set in a grim line. Curious eyes followed her as she crossed the lobby to the front door.

Joe Slocum was standing in the doorway to the bar, staring after the girl. He turned and went back into the bar and let himself out the back door that led into an alleyway, now almost in darkness with the thickening shadows of twilight.

CHAPTER VII

WILL SHEPPARD'S three-roomed log cabin was whitewashed on the outside. A long wide vine-covered porch extended along the front. The big living-room had a large stone fireplace. The kitchen was on one end, the bunkroom at the other. There was a white picket fence around the place and a woodshed and outhouse behind. The bedroom held two bunks. Because this was Brad Rutledge's home when he was in town, his town clothes hung in a separate closet.

The living-room was where Will Sheppard spent most of his waking hours when he was not in a barroom. There were Navajo rugs and tanned hides on the well-scrubbed pineboard floor. A huge handmade table occupied the centre of the room, and was littered with books and tobacco jars and a cigar humidor. A silver tray held a filled cut-glass whisky decanter and a dozen cut-glass whisky glasses, a pitcher of water beside it. Magazines and legal papers were in neat piles. Shep's law library occupied one side of the room, and there were books by Shakespeare, Mark Twain and James Fenimore Cooper. There were half a dozen homemade saddle leather-seated armchairs, and two or three brass cuspidors, all highly polished. An old black leather-bound Bible and a tintype of Will Sheppard's father and mother were on the mantel. It was a man's room, with mingled odours of tobacco smoke and good whisky.

36

The cabin was kept neat and clean by the squaw house-keeper, and the kitchen cupboards were well stocked with food.

Brad peeled off his blood-spattered shirt and washed-up in the leanto outside the kitchen. He put on a clean grey flannel shirt and found the richly coloured meerschaum pipe given him by Shep. He was filling it when an almost timid knock sounded on the door. Brad turned down the wick on the metal Rochester lamp. The room was in shadow when he opened the door. Long practice in an always dangerous country put him behind the heavy door as he opened it. From the narrow crack left in the opening he could make out the shadowy form of Georgia Banning. His pulse quickened as he stepped around the edge of the door.

Georgia stepped in. 'Close the door, quick, and lock it. Somebody has been following me.'

Brad shot the heavy bolt. For a long minute they stood there in silence, so close the perfume of her hair was in his nostrils. She was a head shorter and had to tilt her head to meet his eyes. Both were engulfed in the same sort of embarrassment. Both acutely aware that they stood close together under the same roof, behind doors that were bolted and windows that were heavily curtained. Both wanted to back away, but neither made a move. Both were trying to find the magic word that·would dispel the silent embarrassment.

Brad might have moved his arms a little, or the girl might have swayed towards him. The next moment Brad's arms were around her and with a small faint cry her arms went around his neck. His mouth found hers and they stood like that for a long time. The sob inside her welled and Brad's mouth felt the tremble of it. Then the tears came and wet his face. His knees trembled as he buried his face in her hair. They forgot about the man who had followed her here.

After a while Brad led her to one of the big armchairs and sat down, and she sat sideways on his lap. For the first time they smiled as their eyes met and held. Her fingers caressed his face, his eyes and hair, and her parted lips were smiling, her eyes warm and soft.

'They're sending me away, Brad . . . whether or not my father lives.'

'Why?' The minute he said it he realized he had voiced his own reply.

'Partly on account of you.' She pulled away and looked at him.

Brad pulled her back so that her face was close to his. 'I love you, Georgia. I want to marry you, if you'll have me.'

'I love you too, Brad. You are the only man I ever loved or ever can love. I wouldn't be here otherwise. But I can't marry you and you can't marry me. And for the same reason. That's all it would take to start the shooting. You're a Rutledge. I'm a Banning.'

'I've had that drilled into me till I'm fed up and sick of it,' Brad said. 'If my father wasn't shot and maybe dying, I'd pull out tonight and take you with me. We'd quit the country. Shep would cover our trail, and Chalk would kill anybody who tried to track us down.'

The palm of her hand came down across Brad's mouth. He heard her low whispered words in his ear. 'And I'd go with you to the end of the trail. Somebody's outside.'

She slid off his lap. Brad was on his feet. He cupped his hand over the lamp chimney and blew out the light.

The sound of the shot was loud as the roar of a cannon. The heavy .45 slug spatted as it struck the table where Brad was standing putting out the light.

There was a second shot outside, then another shot, and after that silence. Somebody was rapping cautiously on the window.

'It's me . . . Shep. . . . Let me in the window.'

Brad twisted the catch and opened the window and helped Will Sheppard as he crawled through. Then he closed and latched the window and pulled the blind and drew the heavy curtains.

Shep poured himself a drink.

'Lucky I played a hunch and brought Chalk along,' Shep said as he drank. 'When we heard a shot, Chalk shot twice at a moving shadow, but missed in the dim light. He's on the prowl for whoever fired into the cabin. As long as he's out there, we're safe.'

Shep chuckled drily and poured himself a second drink.

'It's the only time in the somewhat sordid and chequered

career of Will Sheppard that I ever assumed the role of Cupid, and it was almost fatal. And it might well turn into tragedy if you two are found here together. When Chalk gives the all clear signal, he'll escort the lady wherever she wants to go.'

'I'm no lady, Shep. My name's Georgia.' She picked up the flattened slug from the floor and held it in the palm of her hand, looking at it, then she tossed it on the table. 'That almost killed Brad,' she said.

'Nobody but the three of us, and Chalk, and the man who pulled out the chinking in the cabin logs, and shoved a gun barrel into the room, and tried to kill Brad, knew that you two here tonight. I have a hunch that the would-be killer played a lone hand and he'll not tell about it.

'I talked to the doctor and he tells me that both Bob Rutledge and Taylor Banning are too tough to die. They will be back in the saddle before long.

'I have managed to pick up a little cow outfit down on the Missouri river with a few remnant cattle in the KC iron that go with the spread. I'm deeding it to you, Brad. You'll pull out for there tonight, and later Chalk will be down to winter with you.

'I understand, Georgia,' Shep turned to the girl, 'that your father and uncle are sending you away to an unknown destination. They'd rather see you dead than married to a Rutledge.'

'That's right, Shep. The train leaves at midnight. I'll be on it.'

Georgia Banning went over to Brad and took his face in both her hands and pulled his mouth down to meet her lips. Shep went into the kitchen.

'I love you, Brad. Some day, God willing, we'll be married. Until I see you again, goodbye.' She went through the door into the kitchen before Brad could find the words for all that was in his heart. Chalk rapped on the kitchen door and reported all was clear. Shep let Georgia out and told Chalk to escort her to wherever she wanted to go.

When Shep came back into the room, he took an old tintype photograph from his wallet, looked at it for a long moment, then handed it to Brad. 'That girl was once my wife,' he said.

Brad saw the likeness of a beautiful girl about twenty, with dark hair and large dark eyes. She seemed to smile at Brad, and he could tell by the way she had her head tilted that she was proud and courageous. 'Gosh, Shep! She's a thoroughbred!' Brad spoke without thinking, handing the photograph back to Shep.

'Cornelia got it from her mother's side. Her father was a blackleg scoundrel. He sired a son who inherited all his traits.

'Like it is with you, Brad, her father and my father were political enemies, and politics is apt to bring out all that is evil and petty and mean and dirty in men.

'My father, Judge Houston Sheppard, ran against Cornelia's father, Paul Weaver, for Governor of New Mexico. Weaver's only son, Clarence, handled his campaign. When they could not find a black mark on the record of my father, they invented lies about him. But in spite of all the mud-slinging, my father was elected Governor. That night he was shot down, and while there was no way of proving who did the killing, I was willing to risk all I had on earth that the two Weavers were guilty. I was fresh out of law school at the time and working in my father's office.

'Cornelia and I, without knowledge of our parents, had been secretly married for six months. After my father was shot, we announced our marriage in the local paper, giving the date and place the marriage had taken place. I bought a Colt .45 gun and carried it on me, and sent my wife away.

'The newspaper hadn't been off the press very long when Paul and Clarence Weaver came to my house. I was sitting on the porch when they came in the gate. The elder Weaver had a blacksnake whip coiled in his left hand and a .38 pistol in his right hand. His son had his hand on the butt of his gun when they ordered me down off the porch to get the horse-whipping I deserved. Then they'd kill me like they'd killed my father. I'd never fired a gun in my life, but I killed Paul Weaver with my first shot and his son with my second.

'I was sent to prison for that double killing. While I was

there my wife died in childbirth and the baby was born dead. She had no desire to live.

'I'd done five years of a life term when Chalk found me there in the New Mexico pen. He was my cell-mate, and nobody but God will ever know what that black giant did for me. He took me with him, over the prison wall, when he was freed. The law so far has never caught up with me.'

Shep poured himself a stiff drink and held it in his hand, a wistful sort of smile twisting his mouth and his eyes misted. Brad knew that Shep was thinking about the woman he had loved, when he lifted his glass.

'There is something about Georgia,' Shep said softly, 'that reminds me of Cornelia. The brave look in her eyes, the tilt to her chin.' He lifted his glass and drank slowly, in a silent toast. 'I'm going to do what I can to prevent the same thing happening to you two.'

Brad sat motionless, too moved by Shep's tragic story to say a word.

Shep paced the floor a few times, as if something was worrying him. He picked up the flattened bullet from the table and studied it a minute, then flipped it into the air with his thumbnail and caught it. He looked at Brad, his twisted grin cocking an eyebrow. Then he went into the kitchen and when he came back into the living-room he had a service worn cartridge belt, its loops studded with brass cartridges, and a wooden handled six-shooter in a worn holster. He handed it to Brad. 'Buckle it on, Brad. It would seem as if you have incurred the enmity of some man who deals from a cold deck.'

'Ab Adams?' Brad said quietly.

'Abilene, or Joe Slocum. Both about the same height and build. The light was too dim to make identification a certainty.'

Brad buckled on the cartridge belt and felt the weight of the gun against his lean flank. 'I can go through the motions, Shep, but I never was cut out for a gun-slinger.'

'Don't let that enter your mind if the play ever comes up when you have to kill in self-defence. That split-second hesitation might well mean life or death. Remember now, and

41

never let yourself forget it, you have the happiness of the woman you love and who loves you at stake.'

Shep poured himself a drink and sat down with it.

'Bob Rutledge is a ruthless man and a stern father.' Shep spoke quietly. 'He's too damned stubborn-minded to retract what he said to you tonight, too prideful to admit he regrets saying what he did. Chalk tells me that when he walked into the room Bob Rutledge had Abilene Adams covered with a gun, thus incurring the enmity of the deadly and treacherous Abilene. Abilene left the room when Chalk came in, and by the time I got there the argument was over.

'I told Bob Rutledge I was staking you to a cow outfit of your own that I'd bought. I expected him to blow up but he didn't. Without lifting his voice, he simply told me to get the hell out of his room or he would have Chalk throw me out. That seemed to close the incident until Chalk laid your father's cartridge belt and six-shooter on the kitchen table. Your father sent you his gun as a sort of left-handed peace gesture.'

Neither of them felt sleepy. Shep got out the chequerboard and they played chequers for a while. Finally Shep swept the chequers off the board into a box and folded the chequerboard.

'When a man jumps his own king twice in a row,' Shep smiled gently, 'it don't seem like he's got his entire attention on the game. Let's go to bed.'

Even with the light out and each stretched out in his bunk, with neither of them stirring for fear of disturbing the other, it was no go. Shep muffled a cough under the blankets. Brad threw off an extra blanket.

'I've been laying quiet for hours,' Brad said. 'First the sole of my foot itched. Then up between my shoulders . . . maybe I'm lousy.'

'A young buck like you coming down with nerves. Love can do strange things to a normally healthy man. Tell me about her, Brad.'

Shep lay back and smiled in the darkness while the young cowhand spoke, hesitant at first, but once he got started there was no stopping him. He was dreaming it all out and giving voice to his dreaming and Shep was a good listener. When at

42

long last he stopped talking, Brad could hear Shep snoring gently. Brad grinned at himself in the darkness and closed his eyes and was asleep with his second deep breath.

Will Sheppard took Brad to the bank next morning and transferred the title of the KC ranch into Brad Rutledge's name. They met the two doctors who had come from Great Falls and Helena coming out of the hotel. They confirmed the opinion of the town doctor. Both men were too tough to die.

Chalk was staying with Bob Rutledge until he was able to be moved by buckboard to the ranch. Ab Adams had gathered the Block R cowhands and moved camp to the far end of the range for the second round-up. Ab had come back to make peace with the wounded cowman.

Tracy Banning was staying with his wounded brother. Joe Slocum had gathered his BB cowpunchers and left town.

Georgia Banning had been put on the midnight train by her Uncle Tracy, bound for an unknown destination.

Ab Adams had left Brad's bedroll and his string of horses at the feed-yard in town. Brad loaded his bed on a pack-horse and saddled up and headed his string of cowhorses for the KC ranch on the Missouri river. It gave him a strange feeling of freedom to be on his own, headed for his own ranch. He would have made a move to patch up his quarrel with his father, but Shep talked him out of the notion.

It was sundown when Brad herded his horses down the long ridge from the badlands. He had been to the KC ranch before, but now that it belonged to him he saw it through different eyes. The log cabins and log barn and thatched roofed cattle shed. The pole corrals and the big gate in the barbed wire fence that enclosed the ranch. The hay meadows and stack after stack of wild hay and alfalfa. Enough hay to winter more cattle than he ever hoped to own. Enough feed back in the shelter of the badlands to winter twice as many. He could gather enough remnant cattle in the rough country to pay off half what the outfit was worth. KC creek would irrigate the hay meadows, the ditches and cross-ditches already dug.

It looked like Shep had made him a present of one of the best little cow outfits in Montana. One man could, if he

43

worked at it, run the spread. He could hire hay crews, and round-up times he could rep with one of the big outfits that worked the range. That was one good thing about being a little cowman. He was independent. The bigger the outfit the more headaches went with it. Right now Brad had a right to feel prideful. If only Georgia were riding along with him right now he would have been the happiest man on earth.

He slid his tarp-covered bed off at the cabin, turned his horses loose and stabled the horse he was riding.

There was a winter's grub supply in the cabin and dugout celler in the hill behind the cabin.

Brad cooked and ate supper and then went down to the river bank to fish for catfish. He sat there listening to the night sounds. The slap of a beaver tail along the creek that emptied into the river. The boom of a horned owl. The smell of the river and the wild roses in bloom. He sat for a long time without moving a muscle while a bunch of timid white-tail deer went out on the sandbar to drink. Sometimes a coyote yapped. Back in the badlands a wolf howled at the moon.

All this was Brad Rutledge's and all these things belonged to him. The sounds of the night and the pungent odours and the feel of the land. His to share with the woman he loved, God willing. Filled with his dreams, he was content.

CHAPTER VIII

IT takes a lot of gun lead to kill men like Bob Rutledge and Taylor Banning. They were back on their ranches by the time beef round-up was over.

The Bannings had built a seven-wire drift fence between their BB range and the Rutledge Block R. The fence builders had dug post holes along the line Bob Rutledge had surveyed with his fifty-foot reata, using the rock monuments built by Brad and Chalk.

44

Without Brad knowing anything about it, Will Sheppard closed a deal for a little bunch of cattle. He hired a couple of cowhands and they drifted the cattle down through the breaks and on to Brad's KC range. Only Shep and Chalk knew that Chalk's life savings went into those cattle. Chalk had sent word to Brad that as soon as his father was able to sit a horse, he'd be down to winter with him.

'Bet a spotted pony, Mistah Shep,' Chalk had said when they bought the cattle, 'Brad makes us a pile of money from those cattle.'

'Don't let on to Robert,' said Shep, 'that we bought Brad some cattle. He likes to brag how he's glad to be rid of Brad, but there are times, Chalk, when I have a hunch he misses the boy.

'The Bannings are going after Bob Rutledge on this land-grabbing business. They're putting men in on the Block R range, taking up desert claims and buying scrip from the Government. Seen any of those squatters?'

'Yes, suh.'

'Texicans?'

'Yuh knows it. Right from the Banning range in Texas. Gun-toting folks, all of them. Looks like trouble's bound to come. Mistah Bob is limping around on crutches fit to be tied. Swears he's going to bust that drift fence wide open first big snow when the cattle commence drifting. Good winter range south of that drift fence, and them Block R steers is going to need it. Free range, Mistah Bob calls it.'

Will Sheppard nodded. If that drift fence was cut, the Block R cattle would drift into the badlands below, on to land that the Bannings were claiming. It had always been used as winter range by the Block R. Now only BB cattle were down there, excepting for a few wild cattle missed on the round-up. Brad's place was twenty miles below the drift fence.

Shep, in getting the ranch for Brad, had stolen a march on the Bannings, who wanted it badly, as it fringed on their range and could be developed into a valuable line camp. There were acres of wild hay and good feed back in the hills above and down along the bottom land. Now Brad Rutledge owned it. Shep had outfoxed the Bannings, and he had outfoxed Bob Rutledge, who would have paid ten prices for the place.

Brad had heard nothing of Georgia Banning. Alone there on the river, he got little news from the outside. Visitors were few. Brad welcomed the solitude. It gave him a chance to think, a chance to adjust himself to this new way of life away from his father.

He had heard rumours of lawsuits over land and water rights. That the Government and State were going after Bob Rutledge, and that only for the cleverness of Will Sheppard the big cattleman would now be behind bars. Shep had got one postponement after another. He was fighting desperately for time, using every trick in the law bag to save the freedom of Bob Rutledge.

Brad was mending a fence when a buckboard carrying two men came through the gate. One of them, the man driving, was from Alkali. He ran the livery stable there. The other man, in town clothes, was a stranger.

'My name's Markson,' the town man said as they drove up to Brad. 'I'm from Butte. An attorney by profession. I represent a cattle outfit that wants to buy you out. What's your lowest price for this ranch?'

'I'm not selling,' said Brad. 'Not at any price. Who wants the place? The Bannings or Bob Rutledge, my father?'

'I can't divulge the name of my client. I'll offer you twice what it cost you.'

'Nope.' Brad started back splicing his barb wire.

'Three times.'

'Not for ten times what it's worth,' said Brad. 'It's the first real thing, outside a horse and saddle and bed, I ever owned. I'm not selling. Go back and tell that 'to whoever hired you.'

'You're a young fool!' snapped the attorney, angered by Brad's indifference.

Brad straightened up, his fence pliers in his hand. His eyes stared hard at the attorney. 'Get off my place, and get off quick,' said Brad.

'Drive out of here,' muttered the attorney to the driver.

Brad grinned as he watched them drive away without

another word. Then he went back to his fence repairing, whistling as he worked.

It was about a week later that he found a notice tacked to his gate post, printed in red on a board.

'Clear out or you'll be smoked out,' the notice read.

Winter came softly, with big snowflakes that made the world a white blanket. There was no wind. Brad had to get off now and then to knock the packed balls of snow from his horse's hoofs. He was doing some 'rawhiding.' Fetching in poor cattle or cows with late calves. And every time he came back to the ranch with his cows, and perhaps a calf across his saddle, he would notice the sign on the gate. Somebody was paying him visits, but the visits were made when Brad was away from the place. The sign was always the same, and each visit was marked by an empty 30-30 shell left on the cabin table. Two weeks had passed since the visit of the attorney named Markson.

At dusk one evening, as Brad was finishing his barn chores, Chalk rode up. He was dressed in heavy green mackinaw and black and white wool chaps. He was leading a pack-horse that carried his tarp-covered bed.

Brad was never so glad to see a man. Chalk acted like a boy playing hooky from school. He was packing an extra Winchester, which he carried to the cabin and laid on Brad's bunk. Brad looked rather sharply at the giant Negro.

'How come the extra artillery, Chalk?' he asked, as he got the fire going.

'Mistah Shep's idee. He say it's going to be shore bad winter for varmints like coyotes and wolves. He say how yuh-all better get handy with them weapons. He say I better learn you how to utilize them guns.'

'Shep said that? Shep?'

'Yes, suh. Mister Shep say it.'

Chalk washed up and started getting supper. He was as good a camp cook as ever made sourdough biscuits. Behind his wide grin lay news, and Brad waited for it. But Chalk wasn't ready to talk. He sang as he got supper. Now and then he would dance a shuffle. He kept on his belt and gun.

'Chalk, what's up? What fetches you here?' asked Brad impatiently.

47

'Gets my orders from Mistah Shep. Comes here. Me, I dunno what's up. Mistah Shep, he say play my cards careful. He talked big words about sitting on a volcano mountain which is most likely to blow up any day. Where am that mountain, Mistah Brad?'

'Can't say, Chalk. Shep never sent a letter?'

'Shucks, now, he shore did. Done forget what's what when it's grub time. Here's the letter.'

Brad opened it and read it in the candlelight.

'Things are getting serious, Brad. Both the Bannings and Robert are chanting their war songs. You might be dragged into it, so I'm sending Chalk down to stay with you. When the first bad storm comes out of the north, look for trouble. Your father is like a grizzly with a sore paw. The Bannings are playing a mighty clever game and they're out to hamstring Bob Rutledge. They're using the law to do it. Bad sportsmanship on the part of a feudist, I'd say. But so far we're beating them in court.

'Your father is getting harder to handle every day. He even turns at times on the estimable Abilene.

'Brad, Chalk will stand by you. Bank on him in a tight fix. He's an old head at the game so do what he says. Trust nobody else. And if you have to use the guns I'm sending, use them. It will undoubtedly surprise you to learn that Will Sheppard now totes an equalizer in the shape of an old Colt he put away many years ago.

'Keep your guns handy, Brad, and never ride anywhere without Chalk.'

Brad finished reading the letter. Chalk was humming some tune. There was the odour of coffee and sourdough biscuits and frying venison. From outside came the howl of a wolf.

'Chalk,' asked Brad, as he put Shep's letter in the fire, 'how long do you figure on staying down here with me?'

'For keeps, near as Ah can figure.'

'You quit the Block R, Chalk?'

'Ah just naturally up and run off. Saved an argument with Mistah Bob. Just naturally hit a shuck and here ol' Chalk.'

'You mean you're not going back, Chalk?'

'Not while you need me, Mistah Brad. Mistah Shep say

48

we're sitting on that volcano mountain. Chalk gonna sit till she blow up. I tell your mammy long time ago nobody going to harm you while big Chalk can help it.

'I remember the time your mammy nursed Chalk out from the shadow of death when them Bannings shot me up, down along the Mexican border. Yes, Mistah Brad, she nurse this ol' rascal right out from the brink of death. Nursed me twice more when Ah's ailin' with bad fever.

'And so, when she was dying, and she ask me to look after her baby, Ah swears Ah'll always look out for you.

'Shucks, them biscuits is smoking. See what comes of gabbin'?' As the Negro knelt to open the oven door of the little sheep-iron stove his head was bent. A head sprinkled with grey now, and something like a sob shook his heavy shoulders.

Brad's throat choked him. It was hard, right now, to think of Chalk as a killer.

The Missouri river had frozen over from bank to bank, with ice thick enough to cross cattle, by the time the first snow blanketed the cow country. Brad and Chalk built a snowplough. They got up two hours before daybreak and an hour after daylight would find the ground cleared by the snowplough, the overnight freeze of ice cleared on the long trough in the river, and the river ice sanded to prevent the cattle slipping.

Then Brad and Chalk would ride back into the badlands, 'rawhiding.' More than likely they would both ride back with a newborn calf across their saddles, and the mother cows bawling and hooking at their horses' rumps. If it was below zero, and it usually was, they would keep the newborn calves in the cabin while the cows bawled outside. It made for sleepless nights, but it was all in a day's ranch chores in the winter time.

It was a lean day when they didn't brand one or two big yearlings, and even two-year-old mavericks that belonged to the first man that got there.

No man was ever better suited for a snowed-in ranch pardner than Chalk. He could do the work of half a dozen men, for one thing. He insisted on doing all the cooking because he said Brad only spoiled good grub. And while the average cowhand lives on stuff he can cook quickly in a

49

skillet, all greasy food, and baking powder biscuits, Chalk, with nothing but the barest staples to work with and only a small sheet-iron camp stove to cook on, would concoct dishes that Brad had never eaten before. He was always thinking up a new dish to bake in the oven, and always there was a pie or a cake or pudding or a fresh batch of cookies. His five-gallon crock of mincemeat and his chokecherry syrup on thin sourdough hotcakes were something to marvel at, as was the aroma of his coffee as it came to a boil.

But it was the man inside the giant frame, the real Chalk, that counted. Brad came to know him as he had never known any man, not even Shep, who had been his guide, philosopher and friend.

Two men alone in a cabin, sharing all that there is to share together, seldom get along without an occasional clashing of tempers or temperament. Chalk was the rare exception that made the rule. He had brought along his banjo and he would play and sing on the long winter evenings. Songs he made up as he went along. Some sad and wistful, others gay that had to do with animals and birds. Brad would lie back on his bunk and listen while Chalk would assume the character of each animal and bird.

Those short weeks were the happiest days and nights Brad Rutledge and Chalk had ever known. Because while his hair was greying, Chalk was a child inside, and only Brad had ever known the other side of the giant Negro.

Daytimes, when they rode in pairs, Chalk was a different man. A man who was wary and his hand never far from the six-shooter or saddle gun he packed.

But, day or night, Chalk was dangerous. Many a night while Brad slept, Chalk would come awake and slip into his clothes and take his guns and prowl the night. Then he would come back and go back to bed, without Brad ever knowing about it.

Brad had told Chalk about the visit of the attorney named Markson. He showed Chalk the red-lettered warning sign, and told of the visits of the man who always left an empty 30-30 shell on the table in the cabin. But after Chalk came there were no more empty shells left. Chalk had scared the man off. Nevertheless, neither Chalk nor Brad relaxed their vigilance. They were both waiting for something to happen. And when it came it surprised neither of them.

They were in the cabin one night, Chalk picking the battered banjo and singing, and Brad reading a book of Shep's, when they heard the squeak of shod hoofs in the packed snow outside.

Chalk's big black paw swept out the candlelight. Still picking his banjo, he stepped alongside Brad.

'Get fixed. Follow mah play. If it's trouble coming, it's trouble we sell them. Lemme do the shooting. You do the talking. Keep in the dark.'

There was the sound of voices outside, then a pounding on the door. Brad reckoned there were at least two men.

'Who's there?' called Brad, his gun in his hand as he crouched in the darkness. Chalk's banjo was silent now. He was crouched, guns ready.

'It's Taylor Banning. I have a badly wounded man with me. The man needs attention. Open up.'

'Bring him in,' replied Brad. 'Soon as I make sure it isn't a trick, I'll do what I can.'

'It's no trick, young Rutledge,' said Taylor Banning as he opened the door, 'the Bannings don't play tricks.'

Now a match burst into flame as Taylor Banning lit the candle on the table. Then he went outside and helped in a lurching, blood smeared man. He slid the man into a chair, then shut the door and barred it. There was a thin smile on his handsome face as he faced Brad and Chalk. He slid his gun from its holster and laid it on the table, then shed his blood-spattered coonskin coat.

'We'll need hot water and clean bandages,' said Taylor Banning. 'The man's been shot through the shoulder and one leg. Know him?'

'Yes,' said Brad, 'I know him. He's a Block R man.' Brad set about getting a kettle of water heated. Some floursack dish towels, freshly washed, to serve as bandages.

They laid the man on a tarp on the floor. Taylor Banning rolled back the sleeves of his flannel shirt. His left arm was bleeding above the elbow. Chalk sat back in a corner, taking no part. He kept watching Taylor Banning. Chalk had the wounded man's gun that Taylor Banning had given him.

51

'Looks like you can stand some bandaging yourself,' Brad said as he and Taylor ripped off the wounded man's shirt as carefully as was possible.

Taylor Banning's black eyes looked hard at Brad. 'Just a scratch, young Rutledge. The bushwhacker was drunk, I think. I found a half-empty jug in the snow beside him. I should have killed him, I reckon, but he begged like a yellow dog. I didn't know Bob Rutledge was hiring bushwhackers.'

'And yuh-all can bet he never hired one in his life,' growled Chalk.

'This man laid for me and tried to kill me,' said Taylor Banning, ignoring Chalk completely. 'He's a Block R man. I'll get these bullets out of him. The rest of the job will be up to you, young Rutledge. I'll need a sharp knife.'

Chalk, from his corner of the cabin, flipped a long-bladed hunting knife. It struck the table point first, within a few inches of Taylor Banning's hands, where he was making bandages. The knife, stuck in the plank table, quivered. Its blade was spotless, its black ebony handle polished.

Taylor Banning's long-fingered hands were like the hands of a skilled surgeon. Brad and Chalk had to hold down the wounded man while Taylor Banning probed for the bullets. The wounded man, delirious with pain, cursed them all. Chalk fed him raw whisky and held him down while Brad came and went with fresh bandages and warm water and the sterilized knife that had killed, but was now being used to save a man's life.

When the wounded man had been cared for and had gone to sleep, Taylor Banning rolled a cigarette.

'Let me patch up your arm,' said Brad. 'It needs tending to.'

'I'd rather die than have a Rutledge . . .'

Chalk's big fist caught Taylor Banning on the jaw. Banning went down in a heap.

'Get busy, Mistah Brad, before he comes alive.'

Brad bandaged Taylor Banning's arm. Chalk made some coffee and spiked it with whisky.

Taylor Banning sat up after a while and looked at his neatly bandaged arm. He stood up and reached for his gun and coat.

52

'It's storming outside,' said Brad. 'You couldn't get a mile in the blizzard that's hitting us. Looks like we'll have to put up with one another for a few hours.'

'Meaning, I reckon, that I'm a prisoner,' said Taylor Banning, whose jaw ached up into his temple.

'Not that,' replied Brad. 'You've got your gun. The door isn't barred. But the storm is bad and no man or horse can travel far without getting lost. I'm asking you to spend the night, that's all. Take it or leave it.'

Outside the storm howled and moaned. The teeth of a blizzard were biting into the badlands. Chalk had already stabled Taylor Banning's horse and the horse belonging to the Block R bushwhacker.

There was no need to step outside to see that no man or horse could travel far in that storm. Taylor Banning pulled the sleeve of his shirt down over his bandaged arm. He smiled faintly as he looked sharply at Brad.

'Young man,' he said, measuring his words, 'if you weren't a Rutledge, I'd like to have you for a friend. Thanks for the shelter. I'm accepting your hospitality. As a matter of fact I am already in your debt. You saved the life of my daughter, now you offer me shelter from a blizzard. I hope, young Rutledge, that there will never come a day when I'll meet you with a gun in my hand.'

'That goes double, Sir,' said Brad. 'Help yourself to the coffee. Looks like our bushwhacker is going to sleep a month.'

The wounded cowboy was breathing heavily. He moaned in his sleep and muttered through set teeth. Chalk brought in more wood. Outside the blizzard whipped at the cabin. Taylor Banning and Brad sat in a strained silence.

The wounded man finally had to be tied down to keep him from threshing around and opening up his wounds. The slivers of wind that crept into the log cabin made the flames of the two tallow candles gutter.

'Turn in?' asked Brad.

Banning shook his head. 'I'll sit up.' He filled a pipe from a leather pouch. 'This man may need attention. He's in bad shape. You claim the Block R never hired a bushwhacker.

53

Yet this man tried to murder me. I want to hear what he has to say when he comes awake.'

'If he says my father hired him to bushwhack any man,' said Brad, 'he'll be lying.'

'I hope you're right,' said Taylor Banning. 'He was laying for me at the drift fence.'

A silence followed that remark. Brad Rutledge and Taylor Banning and Chalk knew that Bob Rutledge was waiting for the first blizzard to break through the drift fence. He had planned to cut the fence and let through the cattle that would drift down into the badlands. Bob Rutledge had sent warning to the Bannings that the drift fence would be cut between every panel, and that the Block R cattle would winter in the badlands now claimed by the BB outfit.

Chalk kept pacing back and forth in the cabin, his ebony face marked with worry. Brad dozed in his bunk. Now and then the wounded man would mutter in his delirium, and Chalk, a huge figure in red flannel undershirt and blanket-lined canvas overalls and bare feet, his gun shoved in the waistband of his overalls, would stand over him. Taylor Banning, stern-eyed, suffering from his hurt arm, kept smoking his pipe. Outside, the storm beat like some invisible thing, alive, moaning. The candlelight threw distorted shadows on the log walls. Chalk's bare feet pad-padded on the dirt floor, dirt packed as hard as concrete.

'Like a black panther,' mused Taylor Banning, aloud. 'Chalk, you remind me of a black panther, pacing up and down.'

Chalk rolled the whites of his eyes without stopping his monotonous walking. There was something uncannily sinister that gripped the men in the cabin. Taylor Banning consulted his heavy silver watch, which he carried in a chamois pouch. It was three o'clock.

When the wounded man opened his eyes, Taylor Banning bent over him. Brad quit his bunk. He was fully dressed, save for his boots. Chalk stood on widespread legs, looking down at the man. Brad wondered if there was a threat in Chalk's eyes as he stood beyond Taylor Banning and the Block R cowboy. The Negro stood there for the fraction of a moment, then moved aside, giving way to Brad.

54

'Who hired you to bushwhack me?' asked Taylor Banning, when the cowboy had looked at each one in turn.

The wounded man chuckled hoarsely. 'Was it you I took a shot at? I must have been drunk. I was shooting at a grizzly bear. I took one shot when some cuss opened up on me and I must have passed out. I never bushwhacked nobody. I'm just a wild cowboy that gets a cork out of a jug and gargles down too much red-eye. I was bear hunting. Now ain't that just like a fool cowboy to mistake a man for a bear. Looks like I come out on the losing end, bear or no bear. Chalk, I'm dry.'

Chalk brought a tin cup filled with whisky and a dipper filled with water. Brad took them from Chalk's hands.

'When this snake talks, Chalk,' said Brad, 'he'll get his water and booze. Lister, feller, who told you to kill Taylor Banning?'

The man's flinty, bloodshot eyes looked at Brad. Then, with a snarl, he knocked the cup and dipper from Brad's hands. He lay back on the blood stained tarp, an evil grin on his unshaven face.

'I'd heard about you throwing in with the Banning spread,' he said, sneering. 'If I wasn't bad hurt, I'd ask you a few questions. I taken Taylor Banning for a grizzly. He shot me up. That's all you or any man will get out of me.'

Brad had been squatting on his heels beside the wounded man. Now he got up and pulled on his boots. He got into his overcoat and lit a lantern.

'Watch him, Chalk. Banning, you can come along or you can stay, just as you like.'

'Where you going, Mistah Brad?' asked Chalk, his black forehead puckered with worry.

'To the barn and back. I'm playing a hunch. This man heard what we talked about. He's tough and he's dangerous and not as sick as he lets on.'

'I'll go along,' said Taylor Banning, pulling on his coon-skin coat.

At the barn, Brad asked Taylor Banning to hold the lantern. Then he carefully examined the wounded man's saddle. 'New saddle strings of yellow whang leather and a new whang-leather rope strap,' Brad said. 'My hunch is right.'

'What are you getting at, young Rutledge?' asked Banning.

'I'm getting at something that's been on my mind. Before we go back to the cabin, I'm asking you a straight question. I want the right answer.'

'Shoot it, young Rutledge.'

'Did you hire a lawyer named Markson?'

'You mean Ike Markson, from Butte?'

'He's from Butte. Fat. Wears glasses. Has one eye that looks like it was covered with a milky scum.'

'That's Ike Markson.'

'Did you send him here to buy me out?'

'Young Rutledge, if I wanted to buy you out, I wouldn't hire a crooked shyster like Ike Markson to put across the deal. I don't do business that way. Ike Markson is a slimy snake, and the Bannings don't use snakes. Bob Rutledge may need Will Sheppeard, but we don't use crooked shysters.'

'Leave Shep out of this,' said Brad. 'Shep is my friend. I'd fight any man that call him a name. You savvy?'

'I apologize,' said Taylor Banning gravely. 'I spoke hastily. Did Ike Markson try to buy this place from you?'

'Yes, and I ran him off. After that I was warned to quit the country. The man that brought the warnings stole a wide strip of yellow whang leather that I had in the cabin. It matches up with the new saddle strings and rope strap on this saddle.'

'Range rumour has it that you quit your father because of my daughter,' said Taylor Banning. 'Is that true?'

Brad faced Taylor Banning in the lantern light. He nodded briefly. 'Something like that, yes, Sir.'

'My advice to you is to go back to your father. You're his son. The son of Rutledge blood. He'll need you before long. You'd better stand by him. And as for my daughter Georgia marrying a Rutledge, I'd rather see her in her coffin. Young Rutledge, if I ever catch you with her, I'll shoot you down like I'd shoot a mad dog. Is that understood?'

'You said it plenty plain,' said Brad. 'But I'm telling you what I'd tell my father, that if Georgia Banning would have me I wouldn't be scared off by all the guns your feuding outfits pack.'

'What if I dared you to shoot it out here and now?' asked Taylor Banning, his eyes narrowing.

'I left my gun in the cabin,' said Brad. 'But if I did have it and you crowded me into a gun play, you'd never live to get out of this barn. It would be you, not me, that got killed.'

'Meaning, I suppose, that you're a fast gun-slinger?'

'Not me,' Brad grinned, and raised the lantern so that its light shone on a huge shape in the doorway, the figure of Chalk. The lantern light reflected the blue steel of Chalk's drawn six-shooter.

'I reckon,' said Brad, 'we might as well get back to the cabin.'

Taylor Banning looked from Chalk to Brad. The cattleman's black eyes were hard and cruel. He hated the giant Negro.

Brad leading the way with the lantern, they quit the shelter of the barn. The wind drove snow into their faces. It swirled around their legs. A sudden gust of wind blew out the lantern light. They headed for the light that showed in the cabin window, floundering through the black blizzard.

Before Brad took off his cap and overcoat, he went through the wounded man's pockets. He found a jack-knife, tobacco, matches, odds and ends. Then, with a faint grin, he fished three empty 30-30 shells from the man's pocket. The wounded cowboy eyed him in silence.

Chalk made fresh coffee. Nobody wanted to sleep. The bushwhacker lay there, sipping coffee spiked with whisky, his bloodshot, menacing eyes watching them. Every man was wondering about what was going to happen at the drift fence as soon as daylight broke the black sky.

An hour before daylight Taylor Banning showed signs of being restless. With the first crack of dawn he pulled on his chaps and overshoes and coonskin coat.

Chalk looked inquiringly at Brad. Brad shook his head as the Negro started as if to bar Banning's way.

'Let him go, Chalk.'

'Thanks, young Rutledge. You make an interesting host. I'm in your debt.' Taylor Banning fastened the frogs of his fur coat.

'What about me, Banning?' asked the wounded man, sitting

57

up, his bewhiskered face twisted in an ugly grimace. 'Going to leave me here to be murdered by that devil Chalk?'

'Why should I bother about you? I'm going to be busy to-day and I can't stay here to nurse you. I'll send a sled down as soon as the storm breaks. That's doing enough for a Block R bushwhacker.'

'Quitting me, are you, Banning?' the man's voice was a snarling growl. His bloodshot eyes were ugly to look at, killer's eyes, wherein lay lights of treachery and cruelty.

'I made a mistake,' said Taylor Banning coldly, 'when I didn't kill you.'

'You sure did,' snarled the man, laughing crazily. 'You sure did. If Chalk don't kill me, and I get back on my feet, I'll take care of you, Banning.'

'I'll risk that, bushwhacker.' Taylor Banning's hand was on the wooden door latch.

'You were asking me who hired me to lay along the trail,' said the man, 'with a Winchester and a jug of whisky. Just as if you didn't know who's paying me!'

'What do you mean by that?' growled Banning, his face pale.

The wounded man sagged back on the tarp, reaching shakily for his spiked coffee.

'We'll meet up some day, Banning. And you better be ready for me.' He lay back, breathing heavily.

Taylor Banning stood there for a moment staring at the man. Then he lifted the latch and left the cabin.

CHAPTER IX

MAN-MADE plans are fragile things. Fate had intervened to prevent a bloody massacre there at the drift fence.

The BB cowboys, heavily armed and under the leadership of Tracy Banning, were on hand, huddled in makeshift shelters, ready to shoot any Block R man who cut the fence.

58

They had been there since the first hint of dawn, grim-lipped, cold-eyed men from the Texas plains, where many a killer has been born and reared.

North of the drift fence, in a line camp, nearly a score of Block R men waited in vain for the coming of Bob Rutledge and Ab Adams. From the cabin they could see dim shapes of drifting cattle, heads lowered, travelling ahead of the wind-driven blizzard.

Noon, afternoon, then the early winter twilight found them still there in the cramped quarters of the small log cabin. Without the leadership of Bob Rutledge or Ab Adams they were powerless to move. And when the blackness of the night trapped them, they began to wonder if something had happened to their leaders.

While the Block R men sat around on the floor of their warm cabin, the BB gunmen shivered and cursed behind their inadequate shelter. Tracy Banning, in a big buffalo overcoat, rode from one shelter to the next.

'They might be waiting for dark,' he told his men. 'Don't quit your posts.'

'How about grub?' asked one man.

'You'll eat when your job's done.'

'Me,' said one cowboy, 'I could use a quart of redeye.'

'There'll be a keg on tap at camp when the work is done,' Tracy Banning promised them.

Taylor Banning showed up late in the afternoon. His brother scowled at him.

'Where the devil have you been, Taylor?' Tracy asked.

'You'd never guess,' Taylor smiled thinly.

'I sent a man out after you.'

'That was thoughtful of you,' said Taylor acidly, 'but so far in life I've been able to take care of myself. Who's been in charge of this drift-fence business since I've been laid up?'

'Joe Slocum. Thought I told you that I'd let Joe handle the fence business.'

'I want to have a talk with Joe,' said Taylor. 'I want to ask him some questions and I want the right answers. There's a man down at Brad Rutledge's ranch badly wounded. He might die. There's a bullet nick in my arm that he put there. I spent the night at young Rutledge's ranch.'

59

'Who shot you, Taylor?'

'A Block R man. He says his name is Crowe. Maybe you know who he is. He was paid to bushwhack somebody. The light was bad, and he was two-thirds drunk. He opened up on me, and I shot him twice. Then I took him to young Rutledge's ranch near by. Now that man wasn't expecting you or me to be riding down close to the KC ranch. He mistook me for somebody else. I'm wondering who he thought he was shooting at. He wouldn't talk, but he made some queer remarks, just before I left this morning. I'd like to have a talk with our cousin Joe Slocum.'

'You'll find him about three miles down the fence. If it's any of my business, Taylor, how come you were down in that country instead of at the home ranch?'

'Just one of my notions, Tracy. Just an idea. It didn't work out as I expected. I was going down to make Brad Rutledge an offer for his place. Or get him to feed some of our cattle on a percentage basis, maybe. I got shot at and the storm kept me there all night.'

'You'd dicker with a Rutledge?' snapped Tracy Banning.

Taylor Banning smiled. 'I didn't make him an offer. I told you it didn't work out as I expected. No word from the Block R outfit?' Taylor asked.

'I know that their men are at a line camp north of the drift fence. They've been there since last night, but they haven't made a move. I'm betting they'll wait till dark.'

'Dark? With a storm like this! If they don't show up by dusk, call the men off the fence. They can't stand this blizzard for ever. I look for it to storm all night. I'll bet you two to one, any part of a thousand dollars, Tracy, that the Block R outfit don't make a try at fence-cutting this time.'

'Got some inside information?'

'Call it that if you like. I'm banking on it. The Block R men won't make a move without Bob Rutledge or Ab Adams, will they?'

'Hardly likely they would,' agreed Tracy.

'Just before I left the ranch, when it looked like a storm was coming before many hours, the telephone rang. It was somebody calling from town. The man wouldn't give his name, but said that he was willing to lay five to one that no fence would be cut during the storm. Then he hung up.'

'Any idea who was talking?'

'It sounded,' said Taylor Banning, 'like the voice of Will Sheppard.'

CHAPTER X

BOB RUTLEDGE and Ab Adams sat on their cots in a jail cell. The big cattleman was raging with anger. Ab Adams sat on his bunk, smoking thin cigarettes, scowling at the jail wall.

'Get hold of Will Sheppard!' barked Bob Rutledge for the hundredth time as the deputy in charge of the cow-town jail appeared. 'The law has no right to hold us here. Send a man out to round up that whisky-guzzlin' fool. I want action. I want to get out of here.'

'All right,' said the big deputy. 'I'll try to locate Shep. But trying to locate him is like hunting for a needle in a haystack. I'll see what I can do.'

'If you can't find Shep, get a hold of Judge Burkes. He'll straighten this out.'

'The judge has gone to Helena, Bob. Something about the grand jury. Him and the district attorney got called up there on this here same land business they got you bogged down in. You know I'd turn you loose in a minute, Bob, if I had the right. But I can't. My hands are tied. I had to serve those bench warrants on you. You should have been in the court at Helena a week ago. A man's got to do what he's told when he's holding down an office like mine. You should be glad you're in here where it's nice and warm, with that blizzard outside. She's a rip-snorter. Bet she's piling cattle down into the badlands. Bet she'll last . . .'

Bob Rutledge's face was red with pent-up rage. He stood there, big hands clenched, trapped, helpless. Not even Bob Rutledge could break jail.

61

'Get Shep,' he barked hoarsely, interrupting the garrulous deputy. 'Drag him here, if you have to, but get him.'

'I'll do what I can, Bob,' promised the big, slow-moving deputy. 'Here's a quart I fetched over, just in case you needed a drink.'

Ab Adams was on his feet with a smooth, lithe movement. He grabbed the bottle in his lean, clawlike hand. He looked sourly at Bob Rutledge as the deputy walked away. Bob was pacing the short length of the jail cell.

'Just as well take it easy, Bob. Can't do a thing about it,' Ab said, opening the bottle and taking a drink.

'I'll bust out of here if I have to tear the place apart,' growled Bob Rutledge. 'I'll show them who I am. Jailing me for fraudulent land-claiming. Who do they think they're handling, anyhow? And here we got those boys waiting at the line camp, wire-cutters ready, and just the storm we've been waiting for.'

'And Shep's not smart enough to keep us out of jail,' said Ab Adams. 'You better hire a new shyster, Bob. Shep's gone stale on you. He's had a brain, but he keeps it pickled in whisky. Better hire a smart lawyer. Some gent like Ike Markson.'

'Ike Markson?' Bob Rutledge quit pacing the floor. 'The Butte lawyer that won those big cases last year? Kick Shep out?'

'He hasn't helped us much since they put us here last night, Bob. Where is he? Why ain't he showed up?'

'I wish I knew.' Bob Rutledge chewed on a cold cigar. There was a savage look in his grey-blue eyes.

'Give me one guess and I'd say he was drunk somewheres, sitting in a poker game. And us locked up here with that fence deal just right to handle. Bob, Shep's lost his luck. Ike Markson can work him into a knot when it comes to law.'

'Maybe yes. Maybe no. They claim Markson is a world-beater,' replied Bob Rutledge. 'Still, if it wasn't for Shep . . .'

They heard the clang of the outside door, and the sound of footsteps coming down the corridor. Then Will Sheppard stood outside the bars of the jail cell.

'Greetings, Robert. I heard you'd changed hotels. And as I live and breathe, there's the jovial Abilene Adams.'

62

'Where . . . where . . .'

'Calm yourself, Robert. Have I ever failed you? Have I ever misled you? Have I ever deceived you in any way, shape or form? I grieve to see you and the jocular Abilene in the bastille, and I've already made a motion to get you out.'

'Then get the deputy to unlock the door,' shouted the irate Bob.

'My powers of persuasion, Robert, do not extend that far. It takes a court order to free you. And the judge won't return from Helena until Tuesday. All this is a bit irregular, and we'll profit by it when we go before the grand jury. They had no authority to get you in here on a bench warrant. There are one or two other little discrepancies that will tend to strengthen our case. Have patience until Tuesday. This is Saturday. I'll send over the best of food, drinks, whatever you desire.

'Be grateful for the warmth of this friendly bastille, Robert. Outside, the elements are tempestuous. A storm rages. The wind blows. The snow drifts and swirls. Man and beast are suffering in the storm, caught in its icy grip, buried beneath a snowy blanket.'

'You're drunk!' growled Bob Rutledge. 'Drunk as a hoot owl. Get out and don't ever come around me again with your drunken speeches. You're fired. I'm done with you, you whisky-head. I'm sending you back to the pen I snaked you out of. Now get out of here. Tell the deputy to bring me a pen and a telegraph blank. I'm sending a wire to Ike Markson in Butte.'

Shep stiffened. He stood there like a man who had been suddenly, without warning, slapped across the face.

'You mean that, Robert?' he asked quietly.

'I mean it. Clear out.'

Will Sheppard looked at Bob Rutledge. Then his eyes, a little bleak, looked at Ab Adams, who sat there, smoking one of his thinly rolled cigarettes.

'Thank you, Abilene,' Shep said. Then he walked back along the corridor. He delivered Bob Rutledge's message to the deputy, then was let out into the blizzard.

As Will Sheppard made his way up the street through the storm, along the snow-packed plank sidewalk, he stumbled his way along, like a man stricken blind. Under his heavy overcoat his shoulders were stooped. He turned into the first saloon.

CHAPTER XI

At the BB camp south of the drift fence Taylor Banning faced Joe Slocum. A tall, well-made, handsome young cowboy was Joe Slocum. His hair was black and straight, like the hair of the Bannings, but his eyes were pale grey. His features were well made, but when he smiled the smile held no warmth.

Joe Socum was rated as a crack shot, a dangerous man in any sort of fight, and a fast cowboy wherever he was put. He had been expelled from college in his sophomore year for slapping a professor. He had never returned. It had been sort of understood that some day Joe Slocum would marry Georgia Banning. At least, that was what Joe had in mind.

'Joe,' said Taylor Banning, 'you've had charge of the outfit here at the drift fence. I want to know if you hired a man that draws Block R pay, calls himself Crowe?'

'Never heard of him, Taylor. Why should I hire any Block R men?' Joe smiled at the older man.

'I never yet caught you in an out-and-out lie, Joe,' replied Taylor Banning, looking hard into Joe Slocum's eyes, 'but I don't trust you too far. I hope you're not lying about this man Crowe.'

'I know you've never quite forgiven me, Taylor, for monkeying around with those wet cattle down in Texas. But that's several years ago. And I killed those two Mexicans in self-defence.'

'Yeah. Over a cheap little dance-hall girl in Juarez. Took the best lawyer we could get and a lot of money, and no little political pull in Mexico, to keep you from being lined up against the adobe wall and shot.'

'I was wild then. The years change a man.'

'He grows older,' admitted Taylor Banning briefly. 'You're sure you didn't hire this Crowe bushwhacker to kill somebody. Young Brad Rutledge for instance?'

'Did Crowe kill him,' asked Joe Slocum.

'No. But he nearly got me. My horse jumped just in time. Crowe wasn't laying for me, but the light was bad. Almost dark. And he was drunk. I was coming along a trail that young Rutledge had been using when he was out "rawhiding." I think he mistook me for Brad Rutledge. Somebody hired him to do a killing. I just hope it wasn't you.'

'Why should I want Brad Rutledge killed?'

Taylor Banning's eyes narrowed. 'Georgia,' he said curtly.

Joe Slocum laughed shortly. 'In which case, Taylor, I'd do my own killing. I wouldn't hire a bushwhacker to do my private fighting.'

'I'll take your word for it, Joe. Forget it.' Taylor Banning held out his hand, and Joe Slocum took it.

'What happened to Crowe?' asked Joe.

'He's at Brad Rutledge's place. I'm sending a sled down to take him to town. Crowe's wounded pretty badly. He may die.'

'I'd like to go down with the sled. I'd like to have a talk with the gentleman.'

'Go along if you want to.'

Taylor Banning went back into the lighted bed-tent, leaving Joe Slocum standing out in the dark, in the lee of the mess wagon. The darkness hid the faint, grim smile on Joe's face.

Taylor Banning, inside the warm tent, met Tracy Banning's inquiring glance.

'I'm sending Joe down with the sled. He'll go on horseback. I hate not to trust him. He asked to go,' Taylor told Tracy.

The storm was drifting the cattle down into the badlands. The north wind came down from the hills and hundreds of head of cattle were drifting in the blizzard. It was the worst storm in years. At both the Block R and BB camps .men huddled around the stove, for neither horse nor man could buck the storm.

In some places cattle were crowded against the drift fence. Other cattle, storm-driven, piled in on them. They piled up, and those that came behind walked over the frozen carcasses buried in the drifts that covered the fence.

Nature was doing the work that Bob Rutledge and Ab Adams had planned. Nature was covering the drift fence under packed drifts that blanketed dead cattle, allowing the other cattle to drift with the blizzard and find shelter in the badlands.

Chalk and Brad worked desperately, shovelling hay, clearing off the level ground with a snowplough. They made superhuman efforts to take care of the weak cattle and shove on the big steers and strong cows across the river and into the badlands.

They ate breakfast in the dark and were in the saddle at daybreak. They had left firewood in the cabin for the wounded man and left him coffee and cooked grub.

'We'll be back about dark,' Brad told him. 'There's a thousand head of cattle drifting down out of the brakes we have to take care of.'

'Gimme that jug of whisky,' said the wounded man, 'and you can stay away a week.'

Chalk glared at the man. 'Talk, and you get the jug, Mistah Snake.'

'Give him the jug, Chalk,' said Brad. 'He's sick. Let him have it.'

'Ah'd like to make him talk,' growled Chalk, as he put the jug within reach of the wounded man.

The wounded man looked at Brad from bloodshot eyes. Since Taylor Banning's departure the morning before, Brad had kept Chalk from torturing the truth out of the bushwhacker. All he had told them was that his name was Crowe.

'Might be, Rutledge,' said Crowe, 'I'll do some talking when you get back. I'll tell you this much. It was you I was laying for. I was paid to run you off or kill you. I'm glad things turned out this way. You've acted like a white man, and tonight I might tell you a story.'

'I'd like to hear it,' said Brad grimly. 'Don't hit that jug too hard, Crowe. That's all the booze in camp. You'll need it on the trip out.'

They handled cattle all day, a seemingly endless string that drifted with the storm. Chalk, who hated cold weather, cursed the blizzard in a muttered, monotonous undertone as they shoved the cattle across the river.

Snow filled their eyes and nostrils. The wind froze their faces. Their hands and feet were like lumps of frozen clay. But they never quit. The winter day was short and there was work to do. Only when darkness was creeping in on them did they head their leg-weary horses into the teeth of the storm, bound for their home camp. Heads bowed against the wind, they urged their horses across the ice and up the north bank of the river, on across the hay meadow to the barn.

It was just about dark now. As Brad unsaddled, he looked towards the cabin and told Chalk it was odd that Crowe had not lit the light. A feeling of uneasiness came over him and he left Chalk throwing hay to their horses and ploughed his way through the drifts to the cabin.

He sensed that something was wrong inside the cabin. His right hand gripped his gun as he opened the door slowly. Chalk came up behind him, a gun in his hand. He pushed Brad aside and kicked the door open.

Chalk stepped inside and touched a match to the candle. Brad came in. The fire in the stove had gone out, though the cabin was still fairly warm. Lying on his back on Chalk's tarp-covered bed near the stove was Crowe. He was dead. Near him lay the jug, on its side, empty. His bandages had been ripped off and blood covered the man's chest and thigh.

Brad lit the lantern to make more light in the cabin. He bent over the dead man. There was a twisted grimace on the man's mouth. He lay in a twisted position, half off the tarp.

'Looks like he got crazy drunk,' Brad said, 'jerked off the bandages and let himself bleed to death.'

Chalk examined the man, and then said, 'Crowe never killed himself. Somebody done the job for him. His wounds have been gouged open with a knife.'

Looking around the cabin, they could see signs of a ter-rific struggle. An overturned chair, blood spattering the log walls and the dirt floor. And there was a lump and a deep cut on the dead man's head that had not been there before.

'Somebody knocked him on the head, Chalk, then bled him to death,' said Brad. 'The poor wounded devil put up a fight, but he was too much handicapped by his wounds. Whoever did this needs hanging.'

'Listen!'

Chalk was near the door in a single leap, his gun in his hand. Brad stepped in behind the stove, blowing out the candle flame. From outside came the sound of three shots in rapid succession, a pause, three more shots, another pause, three more shots.

'Somebody signalling,' said Brad. He started for the door, but Chalk barred his way.

'Go easy. Might be a trap. Crowe was murdered not more than the three hours ago,' warned Chalk.

Now from a much closer distance came three shots, then a man's muffled hail.

'This way with the sled! I found the barn. This way, men! Halloo, Rutledge! Halloo! Show a light! It's Joe Slocum. We're bringing a sled to carry out the wounded man.'

'Ah'll meet them at the barn,' said Chalk, taking the unlighted lantern. 'Ah trusts no Slocum. Directly Ah finds out what's what, Ah'll light the lantern. Don't open the door till Ah hollers "Open up".'

Chalk's black palm blotted out the single candle flame, leaving the cabin in darkness as he went out.

Brad waited, tense, gun ready. A cold-blooded, cowardly murder had been done inside these log walls. A queer feeling crept up Brad's spine. He was no coward, but there was something stealthy, hidden, deadly about it all.

It seemed a year before Chalk's voice hailed the cabin.

'Open up, Mistah Brad!'

Chalk ushered in three men. They looked half frozen. Brad started the fire. The men were unarmed. Chalk had their guns.

Joe Slocum was saying, 'We're on an errand of mercy. The weather's bad and we're about frozen. Almost lost the trail, the drifts were so bad. Nothing but luck let us get here. How bad is the man wounded?'

Brad pointed to the dead man. 'Looks like you had the trip for nothing, Slocum. The feller's dead.'

Joe Slocum stared at the dead man. Then he met Brad's scrutiny with a faint smile.

'Rutledge,' Joe Slocum said, 'it looks like a murder has been done here. You and Chalk might have to talk fast. I wouldn't want to be in your boots. I'm sending one of my men back in the morning to bring the sheriff and coroner. I'll stay here to see that the body isn't touched.'

From his pocket Joe Slocum took a metal badge. 'Special deputy, Rutledge. I'm the law here in this cabin. You and Chalk are under arrest, charged with murder. You'll have to surrender your guns to me.'

Chalk's blue-barrelled gun slid into view. 'Ol' Chalk ain't giving his gun to no Slocum, and you ain't arresting nobody. You and your men sit down on the floor, and stay there. Come daylight, you can send a man for the sheriff and coroner. Sit down, Slocum, before I knock you down!'

CHAPTER XII

WILL SHEPPARD leaned against the bar, his eyes a little glazed, a tall glass of raw whisky in his hand. He couldn't remember when last he had eaten or slept, except that it was just before he went to the jail to visit Bob Rutledge. That was the second day of the blizzard. Now the storm was over. He turned to the bartender.

'How long did the storm last?' he asked.

'Four days and three nights, Shep. Cleared up this morning.'

Shep thanked him with a nod and sipped the raw whisky. He wondered when Bob Rutledge would strike. When would he come out with the facts of Shep's past? When would he tell the law that Will Sheppard was an ex-convict? When would he bare the facts that would send Will Sheppard to the State prison in New Mexico?

It really didn't matter much, Shep thought. He said aloud, 'All that matters for the present is that the storm is over.' Something of the old sparkle came into his eyes and he chuckled softly.

'Robert and the genial Abilene locked in the bastille for the duration of the storm. You could hear dear Robert roar from here to Jericho when he learned that the charges against him had been faked. When I learned the judge and the district attorney had been called to Helena, I arranged to have bench warrants served for the arrest of Bob Rutledge and Abilene Adams for not appearing in the court at Helena a week ago. I had to do it to keep them from cutting that drift fence and starting a range war.

'Never, never in my whole chequered career have I ever witnessed the equal to that scene when the roaring Robert and the silent Abilene came up in court this morning. Robert roaring blatant threats. Markson, armed with writs and volumes of Blackstone, mouthing threats about the false imprisonment of his clients. Never, even if I go unhung and live to be a million, shall I ever forget it all.

'Another long rye, doctor. Gad, what a court scene!'

'Ain't you had enough, Shep?' asked the bartender.

'Enough? Never enough, doctor, never.'

'There's a room at the back, Shep. Good bed in it. Nobody ever uses it but me. You need some shut-eye. I'll stake you to a pint, and when you get to bed I'll send in some milk toast and a pot of black coffee. You been on a bad one, Shep. You're bedding down if I have to put you to sleep with a bung starter. This is your last rye at the bar. The pint will come in handy when you wake up.'

'Doctor,' said Shep, 'you're a friend in need, but I'm waiting for something. Something of importance.'

'I'll call you if anything turns up, Shep. Come on, now.'

The saloon man half led, half carried Shep to the private back room. He put the weary-eyed attorney to bed, and even before he left the room Shep was dead to the world.

The bartender smiled as he turned the key in the lock and pocketed it. The third rye back had held a few drops of a

70

sleeping medicine the saloon man had got from the town doctor. Shep was good for a sleep that would last at least twelve hours.

Back behind the bar, the bartender polished a glass and held it against the light. He was thinking of Will Sheppard. He liked Shep, despite his faults and failings. Shep was that sort of man. His false gaiety, with a subtle undercurrent of wistfulness, attracted pity. Shep was anything but a well man. With his cough, he was living on borrowed time. He never made denial of the fact that his law methods were not always ethical. He had felt the lash of contempt from more than one judge. Other attorneys snubbed and maligned him, and at the same time feared him.

Time after time, when he apparently was losing a difficult case, he would pull from his bag of tricks something that would win him the decision.

'Will Sheppard,' a great jurist once said of him, 'might have attained the peak of fame. Instead, he sold out for a mess of potage. His is the sort of legal mind that one might compare to the scalpel in the hands of a great surgeon. But unfortunately Will Sheppard neglects to sterilize the scalpel.'

Shep had been sleeping less than two hours when the sheriff brought in Brad Rutledge and Chalk, charged with the murder of Crowe. The saloon man got the news from the sheriff, who dropped in for a hot toddy.

When the sheriff had departed, the bartender concocted a drink and carried it to the back room. Half an hour later Will Sheppard, sober, a little bit shaky, left the saloon by the rear door. At his cabin he shaved, took a cold tub bath, and dressed.

On his way to the jail he met Ike Markson and Bob Rutledge and Ab Adams. He passed them with a quirk of an eyebrow and a twisted smile. They did not speak.

'I'm representing Brad Rutledge and Chalk,' Shep told the sheriff. 'You brought them in. Who's in charge of Brad's ranch?'

'I left three good men in charge, Shep. Men I can trust. Not Banning or Block R men. I've been a peace officer here in Montana for twenty years, Shep. I've known all kinds of

71

men. Brad Rutledge isn't any murderer. He's not guilty, but things look bad. Looks like the deck's stacked against him. You're the only man can clear the boy.

'I felt sore about you getting Bob Rutledge and Adams jailed. And it was only when I studied over the deal that I saw through what you'd done. You had to keep those two from cutting the Banning drift fence and starting a range war, with Brad in the middle of it. It might have cost Brad his life.'

For more than two hours Shep sat in the jail cell, talking to Brad and Chalk, questioning them, jotting down notes, going over the same ground time after time in a studied endeavour to bring out every bit of information that would have a bearing on the case. At last he pocketed his notebook and got to his feet.

'You'll both be better off right in here. Play rummy or chequers for a few days. Keep your traps shut. Talk to nobody. It's a tough case, but we'll lick it. I'll drop in again soon. All you two have to think about is a chequer game, and sit tight. I'll do the worrying.'

In the front of the jail, sitting in the office, talking to the sheriff, Shep found Ike Markson and Bob Rutledge. Shep quirked an eyebrow at them and addressed the sheriff.

'As legal attorney for Brad Rutledge and Chalk I've cautioned them not to talk to anyone. They are to be allowed no visitors without my permission. I'm sending them over a turkey dinner. Take care of them, sheriff.'

Bob Rutledge got to his feet, his face red with anger. He barred Shep's way.

'Kinda high and mighty, ain't you, Sheppard?'

'I'm Brad's attorney, Robert. Any communication you have to make, put it through me. You'll find me at my cabin or at the Silver Dollar saloon.'

Bob Rutledge faced the sheriff.

'I'm Brad's father, sheriff. This drunken bum has no right to do what he's doing. I've fetched a real lawyer to talk to Brad.'

'Perhaps, Markson,' Shep said, 'you forgot to tell Robert that Brad ran you off his place a week or so ago before

72

things began to happen down there. If I were you, I'd stay away from Brad Rutledge.'

When Shep was outside, his mocking smile vanished. He walked briskly down the street to the hotel, not even pausing at the Silver Dollar. A few minutes later he was rapping at the door of Taylor Banning's room. He could hear the murmur of voices inside.

Joe Slocum opened the door. He scowled at the attorney, and said, 'Run along, Sheppard, and peddle your papers. We're busy.'

He would have slammed the door, but Shep's foot was wedged against it. Ignoring Joe Slocum's threatening attitude, he called out:

'If you're a man, Taylor Banning, come out here in the hall. Alone. It's Will Sheppard.'

'Let him in,' said Taylor Banning. Reluctantly Joe Slocum admitted him.

Tracy Banning was sitting on the edge of a bed, pulling on his town boots. Taylor Banning was in the bathroom, shaving. It was a large room, with three beds. Muddy, service-worn boots and overalls were on the floor. Fur coats, muskrat caps, four-buckle overshoes, Angora chaps, fur-lined mittens, gun holsters and cartridge belts littered the huge room that was the town home of the Bannings. A sawed-off shotgun leaned against the wall at the head of one bed and a six-shooter lay on the dresser. There was a half-emptied bottle of whisky on the dresser near the gun.

Shep, without waiting for an invitation, headed for the bottle as Joe Slocum locked the door.

Tracy Banning looked at Shep with cold indifference. Taylor Banning, one half of his face white with lather, an open razor in his hand, stepped out of the bathroom.

'Hello, Sheppard,' Taylor said. 'Help yourself to the whisky and have a chair. I wanted to see you.'

'Thanks. For once we share a mutual wish. Do I drink alone?'

'So far as I'm concerned,' said Tracy Banning, pulling on the tight-fitting boots, 'you'll always drink alone.'

'I'll be drinking in good company,' replied Shep, pouring a generous drink into a water tumbler.

73

'When I scrape this side of my face, Sheppard,' said Taylor Banning in a tone that was just a little too gentle, 'I'll join you. If you can wait.'

'It will be a pleasure to wait.'

Taylor Banning finished shaving and washed his face with a steaming hot towel. When he came back into the room there was no sign of welcome on his face or in his eyes. He poured himself a drink. Standing there in pants and boots and undershirt, suspenders dangling, he raised his glass.

'Here's how, Sheppard.'

'How.'

They drank.

'And now, Sheppard, what fetches you here?' Taylor Banning asked as Shep took a chair.

'A little matter that must be discussed in private,' said Shep, 'or not at all.'

'Very well. I'll be dressed in a minute.'

Tracy Banning grunted as he pulled on his other boot. Then he looked at Shep with a faint grin.

'So Ike Markson has your job of keeping Bob Rutledge out of the pen. Or so I hear,' Tracy said.

'So I've been told,' replied Shep, his left eyebrow lifted. 'Bob Rutledge fired me.' Shep reached for the bottle.

Taylor Banning put on a flannel shirt and tied his tie. He slipped into a coat and buckled on his belt. Deliberately he examined his gun before he shoved it into the tied holster on his thigh.

'Where do we go, Sheppard, for this private talk?'

'We can go down to my cabin,' suggested Shep.

'Don't be a fool, Taylor,' said Joe Slocum, 'it might be a trap.'

'I'll risk that,' returned Taylor Banning. 'If I'm not back in an hour from now, Tracy, look for me in Sheppard's cabin.'

'Do that,' said Shep amiably.

As they passed through the lobby they almost bumped into Bob Rutledge and Ab Adams. The big cattleman glared at the pair, and Shep smiled crookedly. Ab's face was a mask, and his eyes glittered with smouldering hatred. Shep chuckled as he opened the door for Taylor Banning.

74

'The amiable Abilene is perturbed,' he said, as they walked up the street.

When they reached the cabin, Shep made a fire in the stone fireplace. He brought out cigars and opened a bottle of twenty-year-old rye which he poured into the whisky decanter on the table.

Taylor Banning looked around at the orderly, well-kept living-room. He felt at home here as he dropped into one of the big leather chairs in front of the open fire.

Shep filled their glasses from the cut-glass decanter that belonged to a past decade.

'I can't figure you, Sheppard,' said Taylor Banning, looking up at Shep.

'Don't try to. It would be a wasted effort. Here's how.'

'What do you want of me, Sheppard?' asked Taylor Banning.

'I want you to help clear Brad Rutledge and Chalk. I had a talk with them at the jail. They're innocent. That man Crowe was killed by someone else. He was killed because somebody was afraid he'd talk. Have you any idea who might have committed that murder?'

'I'd be a fool to say so, Sheppard, even if I knew. I'll be called upon to testify and I'll have to tell the truth. I'll be compelled to say that Crowe was afraid to be left there in the cabin with Brad Rutledge and Chalk.'

'I'm told that Crowe made some rather peculiar accusations before you left the cabin, Banning. If ever I get you and Tracy and Slocum on the witness stand under cross-examination I'm going to rip you apart. I'll be fighting to save the life of a youngster that's as dear to me as my own son. I'll use every trick I know to clear that boy and Chalk. I don't want you to testify.'

'Why not?'

'Banning, if you testify against Brad Rutledge, I promise to hang Joe Slocum.'

Taylor Banning sipped his drink. 'Sheppard, what sort of a game are you playing?' he asked.

'A dangerous game, Banning.'

'You've broken with Rutledge?'

'Robert fired me. Before he's through, he'll smash me.'

75

'Still you defend his son. Why?'

'You might not understand. It's something a bit finer than the glory I'd get from winning the case. It is not a question of money. It has to do with the brotherhood of mankind, the love of a fellow man. Even a shyster might, inside his heart, have a little atom of loyalty and love for another man.'

'You think a lot of Brad Rutledge?'

'Yes.'

'And you want me to withhold any damaging testimony. Is that the idea, Sheppard?'

'Those are the cards laid out on the table, Banning.'

'I'll play your game, Sheppard. On one condition.'

'Name it,' said Shep.

'I need an attorney on this land business, Sheppard. I'm going after Bob Rutledge. You know enough about his land deals to put him on the rack and pull him apart. I'll help you clear Brad Rutledge and Chalk if you will help me send Bob Rutledge where he belongs. I want to see Bob Rutledge locked in prison. If you agree to be our attorney and send him over the road, I'll see to it that Brad Rutledge goes free.'

'What about Chalk?'

'If I withhold my damaging testimony, there won't be much against Chalk. You can clear him. How about it, Sheppard?'

Will Sheppard set down his empty glass. He picked up Taylor Banning's hat and handed it to him. Then he opened the cabin door.

'I've dropped rather low in this world, Banning,' Shep said without heat, 'but not low enough to doublecross a man who has befriended me. You erred in your judgment of Will Sheppard. Get out of here, Taylor Banning.'

Taylor Banning stared hard at Shep. 'Sheppard, you're shoving your drunken head into a noose. I thought you were smart. I find you are just a whisky-guzzling fool. I'll send Brad Rutledge to the pen. I'll hang Chalk. And you'll be in prison with Bob Rutledge before I'm done with you.'

'You've taken on quite a job, Banning. You're biting off a big hunk of meat. Watch out that you don't choke. Now get out!'

76

CHAPTER XIII

In the jail cell, Shep sat on Brad's bunk. He slid a thin package under Chalk's blankets. When he spoke, his voice was barely audible.

'You know how to use those hacksaw blades, Chalk. You go out tonight and back down into the badlands. Don't kill anybody unless you're crowded. There's a fast horse and guns hidden in the brush. Chalk, you're outlawed from now on. You'll travel the hoot-owl trail till I call you in. I want you to trail Joe Slocum and Ab Adams. Never mind the Bannings or Bob Rutledge.'

'Can't I go with Chalk?' asked Brad.

'No. I'll need you here. Chalk, you tie Brad up, and gag him. Then make your getaway. You're guilty of murder. You killed Crowe. Brad is simply the innocent victim of circumstances. You'll keep on being guilty of Crowe's murder until I call you in. Later on I'll clear both of you.'

'But Shep,' Brad protested, 'I can't let Chalk take all the risks. Why can't I . . .'

Shep's voice cut in with the sharpness of a razor blade. He lost none of his calm, but his words were voicing a pent-up emotion.

'Chalk and I have been through a lot of places, Brad. We're older than you are. I'm bossing this show. Chalk goes away tonight. You stay here, and when the time comes you'll come up for trial. If Chalk came up at the same time we'd be licked from the start. Don't you trust me, boy?'

Brad nodded. 'All right, Shep. But it sure makes me feel like I was a coward.'

Shep smiled twistedly. 'Chalk's end of it is the easier part. You're going to hold down the hard end of the job when you come up for trial. That right, Chalk?'

'Yes, suh, Mistah Brad, Mistah Shep he's right. Sho' is!'

77

Shep stayed there talking for half an hour, then went to the hotel. Ike Markson followed him into the barroom adjoining the hotel lobby.

'I'd like to see your files, Sheppard, and check up on the Rutledge land. Dates, surveys, all the scrip and leased land. It's in a jumble. Rutledge is in a tight spot, and I must have your co-operation to get anywhere.'

'What are you willing to pay?' asked Shep.

'Pay? For papers that belong to my client? Why should it cost me or him a thin dime, Sheppard?'

Shep's left eyebrow lifted. 'I asked a question. How much am I bid for the information and papers you need?'

'Not a dollar, Sheppard. You can't bluff me.'

'I wouldn't step out of my tracks to bluff you. I don't need to. You don't see my files, Markson. You get no information from me.'

Markson glared at the smaller man. Big, oily, swarthy, he clenched his fists. The slender Shep smiled faintly.

'If I were you, Markson, I'd keep my temper under control. Of course, you could knock me cold with one punch. It's been done by smaller men than you. But it won't buy you much, Isaac. The bartender here happens to be a friend of mine. If you've never had a bung starter bounced off your head, then I'd advise you to lay off any sort of violence.

'Run back to the man that got you your job with Bob Rutledge. Tell Abilene Adams you couldn't get what you wanted. Tell him that Will Sheppard don't sell out to any man. Tell him that before I'm done with him he'll wish he'd dug a hole, crawled into it, and pulled the hole in after him.'

Markson left without saying another word.

Chalk sang in a deep, rich-toned voice as he and Brad sawed through the jail bars. There was a white moon outside and Chalk rode into the night.

He left Brad alone in the cell, bound hand and foot and gagged. Brad was thinking about his ranch down on the river, and the cattle to be fed. He thought of his father and Ab Adams and Shep, of the Bannings and Joe Slocum and the murdered Crowe. He wondered where Georgia had gone and if he would ever see her again.

The hours until dawn seemed endless. The deputy in

charge of the jail looked in a time or two, but Brad made no sound. Chalk's bunk looked all right. The blanket covered a hump made by the pillow and extra bedding. The sawed bars were back in place.

Breakfast time brought the deputy in. Brad's arms and legs were numb and swollen from being tied. The gag had rubbed his mouth raw. When the deputy released him, Brad told him that Chalk had tied him up, sawed the jail bars and high-tailed it.

The sheriff got to the jail about the same time Shep showed up. Shep needed a shave and sleep. He had a haggard look.

'Looks like I've lost a client, sheriff,' Shep said.

'Shep,' growled the sheriff, 'why don't you just sit down and bust out crying? From now on I'll have you searched before you get inside this jail. You know what this'll cost me at election time. It will lick me. The Bannings will see to that.'

'Keep your shirt on, sheriff. A lot is going to happen between now and election time.'

'I'm swearing out a warrant for Chalk.'

'Sheriff, Chalk didn't kill Crowe. Chalk don't kill crippled men. Go after him if you think it will do any good. But I'm telling you it won't. You can't find him, so take things easy.'

Shep told the sheriff that he was asking the judge to have Brad Rutledge brought up for a hearing this morning.

'Figure you can get the boy off?' The sheriff's tone was no longer gruff. He knew that Shep had brains, that Shep seldom made a wrong move in his game.

'Taylor Banning's testimony will put Chalk in a bad light. But there won't be enough concrete evidence to hold Brad, now that Chalk has flown the coop. It will look like Chalk is guilty. They can't hold Brad except as a material witness, and I'll spring him on bond.'

'The bond will be a high one, Shep. Who'll furnish it?'

'I'll attend to that,' said Shep.

Bob Rutledge, in his hotel room, eyed Will Sheppard coldly. 'What fetches you here?'

'Brad needs someone to go his cash bond, Robert. Are you willing to put up the boy's bond money?'

'Shep, I told you I was going to smash you. You quit me

in a tight corner. Brad quit me when I needed him. What I said goes as she lays. I'm not putting up any cash bond for a lot of quitters. I'm fighting the Bannings, and I'll lick them, without your help. No true son would turn against his father like Brad did. Chalk showed a yellow streak. You turned traitor on me. Now you got the nerve to come here and ask me to go Brad's bond. Get out!'

'That's final, Robert?'

'That's final,' growled Bob Rutledge.

'If I know anything about human nature, I'd say that Brad would rather hang than accept anything from you now. He didn't know I was coming here. I won't tell him.'

Shep left the hotel and walked down the street to the sheriff's office. Shep did a jig step, and smiled. 'Everything is lovely, and the goose hangs high. When the court opens in the morning Brad's bond will be posted.'

'Glad to hear it, Shep,' said the sheriff.

'Any news from the badlands?'

'The posse lost Chalk's trail. Want to see Brad?'

'I'll be back later, sheriff. Have some business to take care of. Tell Brad everything is fixed.'

Shep went back to his cabin. He took a drink to steady his nerves, then lay down, fully clothed, on his bed, setting his alarm clock for eight-thirty.

The alarm brought him out of a dreamless sleep. He washed his face in cold water, brushed his hair, and pulled on his overcoat. Then he walked over to the jail.

The moon was a round white disk. The stars were like diamonds sprinkled on black velvet. Underfoot was a white blanket of snow.

The stove inside the sheriff's office was cherry-red. The sheriff was dozing in a swivel chair behind his desk. He blinked his heavy-lidded eyes, then his jaw dropped. He was looking into the black muzzle of a long barrelled .45. The man who held the gun was masked and wore a long overcoat.

'Lift 'em high,' sounded the muffled voice behind the heavy black silk muffler that served as a mask. 'High, or I'll kill you!'

The sheriff obeyed. 'What do you want?' he growled.

'Never mind. Put your hands around behind your back and lay down on the floor.'

As the sheriff whirled, a gun rapped him across the head. He went down in a limp heap. The masked man tied him hand and foot and was convinced he would stay asleep for an hour or more. Then he scribbled a short note on a yellow pad.

'We're taking Brad Rutledge for a horseback ride. Follow us and you won't get back,' he wrote in a scrawling hand.

He left the note on the sheriff's desk, with the sheriff's keys, after he had unlocked Brad's cell.

Shep told Brad to never mind asking questions. He handed Brad the sheriff's fur coat and cap and gave him his gun. He told Brad to meet Chalk at the old cabin on Wild Creek. It was a hidden cabin in a deep canyon that Shep had found out about from some outlaw. He instructed Brad how to get there.

Ten minutes later Brad Rutledge was riding through the white winter night. It was good to be free once more. But what had happened? Shep had promised Brad that he'd get him out of jail under a posted bond. Now here he was with a carbine and a six-gun, and Shep's parting words in his ear.

'Hide out with Chalk, Brad, till I send you word. Chalk knows what to do. He'll meet you along the trail to the hidden cabin.'

Shep, in a corner of the bar-room, was dozing over a half-emptied bottle of whisky when the sheriff and a deputy came in. The sheriff shook the attorney awake.

'They've taken Brad Rutledge, Shep,' the sheriff growled.

Shep came awake with a visible effort. His eyes were bleary.

'What about Bob Rutledge?' he muttered.

'Not Bob Rutledge. It's Brad. They sprung him about three hours ago. Knocked me on the head, and got my keys.'

Shep jerked to his feet unsteadily. He took a drink from his bottle, hanging on to the table with his other hand.

'Sheriff,' he said drunkenly, 'this is no time for practical joking. Let a man sleep. Brad's going out in the morning on a cash bond.'

81

CHAPTER XIV

AT a small log cabin on Wild Creek Brad and Chalk hid out. They never skylighted themselves, and were always on the watch. Each of them had powerful field glasses, from which they watched Brad's ranch.

Shep paid them a visit one night after dark and left before daylight. They were glad to see him.

'Your popularity is increasing,' he told them, 'the strata of life called society has increased the value on your lives. They're offering five thousand apiece for you.'

'Dead or alive, Shep?' Brad grinned.

'Dead or alive. Preferably dead.'

'How's dad, Shep?'

'He's still the same as ever. I arranged to have both him and the Bannings put under a heavy peace bond. They check their artillery with the sheriff when they come to town. But on the open range they can do as they like. I look for trouble.'

'You're not telling me all of it, Shep.'

'No,' admitted Shep, 'I'm not. You and Chalk do your job. I'll take care of mine. Now tell me what you've seen through the field glasses down at the ranch.'

'Like you told us to, Chalk and I cut the drift fence apart. There's ten thousand head of BB and Block R cattle on the south side of the river. They'll winter, barring another bad blizzard. The feed over there is good. The stout cattle can rustle and the snowploughs are working all day for the weaker critters. The water holes are all kept open. But who's footing the damages?'

'Don't let that worry you, Brad. It's a hard winter. It would take all the cowboys in Montana to drift those cattle back. The Bannings and Bob Rutledge will get a bill for the damages when the Chinook wind cuts away the drifts and the grass comes up again in the spring. You leave the thinking to Shep.'

'But listen, Shep. What are they going to do to my father on this land business?' asked Brad.

'They have an idea, Brad, that they'll nail him to the cross. The Bannings are closing in on him.'

'Can't Ike Markson clear him?'

'Ike Markson, Brad, couldn't clear Bob Rutledge, even if he wanted to. And he don't want to.'

'What do you mean, Shep?'

'Some day, in a few months, Ike Markson is going to try to pull some irons out of the fire. When he does, he's going to burn those soft, fat, white hands of his.'

'I wish you'd tell me what it's all about, Shep.'

'I'll handle it, Brad. The Bannings and the Block R cowboys can't do much until the snow is off the ground. They're snowed in. They're riding out one of the hardest winters Montana ever saw. That broken drift fence saved both outfits. They'd both have lost thousands of cattle if you and Chalk hadn't cut that spite fence. Your hay is feeding BB cattle and Block R cattle. At forty dollars a ton. I might raise the price to fifty.'

'What do you mean, Shep?' asked Brad.

Shep's left eyebrow lifted. He sipped his black coffee, spiked with whisky.

'You'll find out, Brad, when the Chinook wind cuts the snowdrifts and melts the ice on the Missouri. Well, it's time I got going. Daylight in two hours.'

'But it's snowing hard, Shep,' protested Brad.

'Brad,' said Will Sheppard, 'when it's snowing, the snow has a habit of blotting out tracks.' Shep put on his fur coat and cap and overshoes.

It was on Christmas Day that Shep paid them a second visit. He brought some strings for Chalk's battered banjo and a jug of whisky and some canned stuff. Chalk made a suet pudding known as a 'son of a gun' in the sack. They had beans and beef and biscuits.

The storm was one of those blanket snows without wind. The attorney, a little frostbitten, got to the hidden camp an hour after dark.

After they had eaten heartily, Brad asked Shep about the hidden cabin on Wild Creek. He figured it was an old outlaw camp.

'It was once a hide-out for outlaws. The place belonged to a horse thief. He had a few mares, and raised horses. But his real job was to furnish certain men with horses, grub, cartridges, guns, or whatever they needed. It's the safest place to hide that a man could find,' Shep told him.

'It's been safe for us, Shep. Nobody's bothered us.'

'No. Nor they won't, Brad. You and Chalk are set for the winter. Nobody will come here.' Shep smiled faintly as he sipped his coffee. Chalk was softly strumming his banjo and listening to Shep talk.

'See those initials carved on the door? Those outlaws wintered here some years ago. Four of them. When all the law officers in the country were trying to track them down. As you know, there is only one way in here, one way out. They always kept a man on guard there where the trail drops down between the rock walls of the box canyon. There's a man on guard there now. When you and Chalk go up there to watch your ranch below, your sign going in and out is lost when you cross that rock ledge. And even if anybody tried to find you, there would be a man to stop him.'

Brad could easily understand why Shep had picked their hiding place.

'Any news about dad?' Brad asked.

'Robert comes up next week, Brad. Special session of the grand jury in Helena. If the Bannings prove what they hope to prove, your father goes to prison for an indefinite term.'

Brad paced the floor for a long time. Chalk and Shep kept watching him covertly. Now and then the attorney and the Negro exchanged meaning glances. Finally Brad halted in front of Shep, who was pretending to read a book.

'I'm pulling out in the morning, Shep,' he said.

'For where, Brad?'

'Home. My dad needs me. He's standing alone.'

'How can you go home, Brad, when there's a bench warrant out for you? When there's five thousand dollars bounty on your hide? What good could you do? How long would it be before the law caught up with you? Brad, you can't go

84

anywhere until I give you the signal. When the time comes I'll give you your chance. But until I say so, you're stuck here with Chalk.'

The next day Shep was gone. Brad was unwrapping some woollen shirts the attorney had brought him. As he unfolded the newspaper wrapping a headline of a month old struck his gaze like a blow across the face. The article read:

'Attorney now Fugitive. Will Sheppard wanted by the law. Attorney Ike Markson has made astounding accusations against Sheppard, who for many years has been so closely connected with the cattle baron Bob Rutledge. Sheppard has vanished. It is believed he is headed for New York as he purchased a one-way ticket for that city.

'Bob Rutledge has refused to give out any statement regarding the charges against his former right-hand man. In fact, he was a bit rough on the newspaper men who called at his ranch house for an interview.

'Bob Rutledge himself is in a bad spot. Despite the suave assurance of Ike Markson, public opinion is betting that Bob Rutledge will lose out when he's put on trial for fraudulent land grabbing. The Banning brothers are pushing the case hard.

'Abilene Adams, Rutledge's foreman for many years, was as loquacious as the proverbial clam when interviewed. Never at any time a talkative man, Adams' lips were more tightly sealed than ever.

'The authorities are still searching for Brad Rutledge and the Negro, Chalk. Since their spectacular escape from jail a few months ago they have not been seen.

'What has become of Will Sheppard?'

Sitting there on his bunk, Brad thought back along the years, recalling the little things that Shep had told him, and now that he knew something of Shep's history those little things took on a new meaning for him. He began to understand the man.

Brad roused himself from his thoughts and a flat grin spread on his black stubbled face.

'Bob Rutledge will come up for trial in a few days and Will Sheppard is going to defend him, in spite of all that my father has done and said. Ike Markson has dug up Shep's

85

back trail and is using Shep's prison record as a club. It takes a hell of a lot more than that threat to scare Will Sheppard off.'

'You can say that twice, Mistah Brad.'

'I've got a hunch Shep is at the Block R ranch right now. Having it out with my father. In order to act as Bob Rutledge's attorney Shep will have to give himself up to the law.'

'Mistah Shep done give himself up to the sheriff a long time ago,' grinned Chalk. 'Mistah Shep and the sheriff come to some agreement.'

'Shep wanted me to know what there is to know,' said Brad. 'And now that I've found out, let's get going, Chalk. We're backing Shep's play if we have to go back to jail to get the job done. We're heading for the Block R ranch. It's time my father and I had a showdown.'

It was an hour or so before daylight when they rode up to the Block R ranch. A light burned in the cookhouse. Another light, hidden by tightly pulled blinds, showed in the big house where Bob Rutledge lived. Brad and Chalk left their horses in the lee of the big barn.

Through the shadows they made their way to the house. They could hear the sound of voices, thick with whisky, raised in uncontrolled anger.

'I'm betting that Shep's in there and that he's in a tight corner, Chalk. We'll play the cards that's dealt us,' said Brad.

Brad had a key that fitted the back door, and they went in that way.

From the front part of the house they could hear Bob Rutledge talking. 'I would have taken you and the kid back, Sheppard, but you threw in with the Bannings. I don't like traitors. There's only one kind of medicine, lead poison, that does them any good. I'll give you an even break when it comes time to take your medicine.'

'I'd like to do my gun fighting with our friend Abilene, not you,' said Shep quietly.

'You quit me, Shep, when I needed you. I'll take care of my own cards. Ike, give him a drink. He needs it.'

'I'd rather choke from the lack of it, Robert, than touch my tongue to whisky Ike Markson poured out. I came here to kill Abilene Adams. Where is he?'

Shep's voice broke into a racking cough. Ike Markson laughed.

Brad and Chalk, crouched in the hallway, heard the thud of a hard fist, a whining groan, the thump of a body on the floor. Then came Shep's voice, a husky, broken whisper.

'Thank you, Robert.'

Brad walked into the room, his gun in his hand, his blue-grey eyes ablaze. Chalk stalked behind him. They saw Shep sitting in the chair he always chose when he came to the ranch. They saw Bob Rutledge, in a heavy flannel under-shirt and blanket-lined overalls, suspenders hanging, fists clenched, legs wide apart, standing over the whimpering Ike Markson. Bob Rutledge was glaring at the whining lawyer. Shep was wiping blood from his mouth.

'No man,' said Bob Rutledge hoarsely, glaring down at Markson, 'can laugh at Shep and not pay. Get out of here, Markson. Go back where you belong. No man can laugh at Shep when he's . . .'

Bob Rutledge whirled as Chalk, with an ugly chuckle, pushed past Brad. He faced Brad, who stood there, white-lipped, a gun in his hand. For a long moment that seemed eternity, Bob Rutledge stood looking at Brad. Brad's right hand shoved his gun back into its holster and he held his gun hand towards his father.

'Why, you . . . you . . . Brad! You've come home!'

'I've come home, Dad.'

Brad was crushed in the bearlike embrace of his father, big racking sobs coming from the big man's throat.

Chalk picked Ike Markson up bodily and threw him out-side. When Markson had ridden away and the happy reunion of father and son was over, Bob Rutledge told Shep that it was Abilene Adams that talked him into hiring Ike Mark-son, but that thanks to Shep he had got rid of him and Shep was back. He would need Shep now. His trial was coming up next week.

Shep tried to scold Brad for not staying at the KC ranch, but now that Brad and Chalk were here he'd have to arrange bail bond for them. Bob Rutledge spoke up and said he'd give Shep the money for the bond.

CHAPTER XV

BOB RUTLEDGE, poker-faced, grim, sat in his chair in the crowded court room. The law was trying to prove the cattleman guilty of fraudulent land stealing. The trial was being held at Helena, the State capital.

Bob Rutledge's cold-eyed stare swept the crowd. A few of his Block R cowhands, hand picked for their cool-headness in a fight, were scattered through the court room. There were a few cowhands from the Banning BB outfit. The sheriff had sprinkled a few of his special deputies around the court room to maintain law and order.

Across the aisle from the prisoner's dock sat the prosecuting attorney. With him sat Ike Markson, and behind them were placed three empty chairs. The Bannings had hired Markson to help the prosecuting attorney send Bob Rutledge to prison.

Will Sheppard, freshly barbered, clad in a new tailored suit of salt and pepper material, a new white broadcloth shirt and maroon coloured tie, a red carnation in his buttonhole, was to all outward appearances sober. He entered the court room carrying a brief-case under his arm. He eyed Ike Markson as he passed him, with a raised eyebrow, and said, 'I trust you are in excellent health, Isaac. That your heart will stand the strain.' The low mockery of his voice carried to the far corners of the court room.

A pair of dark glasses partly concealed a black eye on Ike Markson's oily, fleshy face that now flushed darkly. The black eye left by a single blow of Bob Rutledge's big fist.

A chuckle spread like a ripple across the court room. They knew Will Sheppard by reputation only. Now Shep had fired the opening shot.

Shep walked over to his own side of the court room. He

opened his brief case and took from it a coiled rawhide reata and held it in his hand. The brief case gaped open and empty save for the rope. He laid the reata on the table, then tossed the empty brief case aside and took his seat.

Brad Rutledge and Chalk had come in through the door behind Shep. They walked side by side and close together and a deputy sheriff followed them. They were handcuffed together. It had been Shep's idea, and he had slipped a spare key to fit the handcuffs into Brad's shirt pocket. Brad and Chalk settled themselves in heavy armchairs near the prisoner's dock, next to Shep. They were now free on bail bond.

Brad sucked in his breath when Taylor and Tracy Banning came in by the front door. Between the two men walked Georgia Banning, wearing a plain black tailored suit and a black Stetson hat. She carried her head proudly, looking straight ahead.

Ike Markson was on his feet, opening the low gate that separated them from the audience. Taylor Banning brushed the attorney aside and held the gate for Georgia to pass through. She cast Brad a quick look, giving him a faint, fleeting smile.

Shep reached over and gripped Brad's leg under the table. 'Steady, son.' Shep's voice was barely audible in Brad's ear. 'She's part of the stage setting. The Bannings were fit to be tied when Georgia showed up at the home ranch.'

Brad's heart was pounding the blood up into his throat.

'I don't get it, Shep. You mean you knew where she was all this time and never told me.'

'You're beginning to grasp the idea, son. Not even her father nor Uncle Tracy knew her whereabouts. She slipped off the train at the town I told her about. She got in touch with me and we've been in communication ever since. Yonder sits a real lady, Brad.'

'Order in the court!' The baliff rapped for silence. 'Hear Ye! Hear Ye! This court is now in session!' he droned as the jurymen took their seats in the jury box.

The prosecuting attorney was a young man with political ambitions. Fired by political zeal, and with the backing of the Banning brothers, and the damning evidence gathered by Ike Markson, the prosecuting attorney felt sure of winning his case. He had every reason to be sure of himself. Legal proof was there within the red-inked boundaries marked on a huge land map he had in front of him. Sections of State and Government land Bob Rutledge was claiming without legal benefit.

To back up his claims of fraudulent land grabbing, the prosecution had Tracy and Taylor Banning for witnesses. Eye witnesses who had watched Bob Rutledge, Abilene Adams, Chalk and Brad Rutledge, and Will Sheppard, the attorney for the defence, survey the land Rutledge claimed. Travelling on horseback with a map from the land office and a rawhide reata.

Never had a prosecuting attorney come into court with a more airtight case. It was a foregone conclusion that Bob Rutledge would be sent to prison.

The tall, blond, clean-shaven, immaculately tailored young prosecutor got to his feet to make the opening address to the court.

'I intend to and will prove beyond all shadow of a doubt that Robert Rutledge claims ownership of State and Government lands that do not legally belong to him. Robert Rutledge illegally surveyed those lands and water rights, and in claiming the land he is subject to imprisonment for grand theft.

'The prosecution will prove that survey illegal, and prove that the parties involved in said illegal survey are subject to a violation of the laws of Montana.'

The prosecutor paused, his sweeping glance taking in the judge and jury and the crowded court room.

'Your Honour, before continuing I would like to file protest. The attorney for the defence, Will Sheppard, has a prison record, and is even now an escaped convict. On those grounds I protest his legal right to practise law in the State of Montana.'

A low murmur sounded in the court room, then a hushed silence.

'Objection overruled,' said the judge. 'I have here before me all records concerning Will Sheppard's past, and the full pardon from the Governor of New Mexico. This pardon has been waiting for Will Sheppard since the day he made his

90

escape from prison. He gave himself up to the sheriff here, who got in touch with the authorities in New Mexico. Will Sheppard has the right to stand before this court in a legal capacity.'

The young prosecutor took a white silk handkerchief from the breast pocket of his coat and dabbed at the beads of perspiration that had formed on his forehead.

'Your Honour,' he continued, 'Brad Rutledge, witness for the defence, stands accused of a brutal murder. On those grounds I move that his testimony be stricken from the court records.'

The prosecuting attorney gave Brad a hard look, and sat down.

Will Sheppard rose to his feet. Adjusting the red carnation in his buttonhole, he said:

'Your Honour, Gentlemen of the Jury. In defence of myself and my name, I stand before the mercy of this court of justice. It is true that I have a prison record. Years ago I shot and killed two men who needed killing. I served five years of a life sentence, then escaped prison. I gave myself up to the law in order that I might defend in this court a friend of long standing, not then knowing that my full pardon was waiting for me.' Shep bowed stiffly, making a small gesture with his hands. His eyes swept the jury box when he spoke again in his quiet voice.

'Your Honour, Gentlemen of the Jury, and Mister Prosecutor, I wish to state now that the defence has no intention of putting Brad Rutledge on the witness stand. It would seem that my over-eager opponent has, to use a familiar term, jumped the gun.'

Shep fingered the red carnation, tilting his head a little sideways to smell its somewhat potent odour. His eyes were fixed on Georgia Banning now. On the red carnation she wore pinned to the lapel of her black coat.

The judge, the men in the jury box, the men in the packed court room, saw Georgia Banning smile into the eyes of Will Sheppard. They had missed nothing of the little theatrical touch. On either side of Georgia, Taylor and Tracy Banning stirred uneasily, scowling, glaring down at the red carnation she had taken from her bag and pinned to the lapel of her coat.

Brad was staring, puzzled, when he felt Chalk's big hand tug gently at his handcuffed wrist.

'That Mistah Shep, smartest man alive,' Chalk whispered, a soft chuckle cushioning his words.

Shep sat down. He poured half a tumblerful from the half-gallon water pitcher that contained a colourless liquid.

'Your Honour, Gentlemen of the Jury, the defence rests.' Shep had the feeling that the judge, jury and the court room crowd were on his side.

The prosecutor's table was piled with law books. Ike Markson had a pile of legal papers in front of him. While the young prosecutor, a long schoolroom pointer in his hand, pointed out to the judge and jury the various tracts of land claimed by Bob Rutledge, Ike kept consulting his various documents and whispering in the ear of the prosecuting attorney.

There followed long hours of dry, boresome facts while the prosecutor built up his case, step by step, against the accused cattleman.

After he had the judge, the jury and the majority of the crowded court room convinced beyond the remote shadow of doubt regarding the guilt of Bob Rutledge, he put Tracy Banning on the witness stand.

'Did the accused, Robert Rutledge, ever threaten you and your brother in any way when you met him the day he was completing his survey?'

'He sure did. He said to get the hell off his land or he'd kill us.' Tracy Banning added his damning testimony, and was excused.

Taylor Banning took the witness stand and corroborated the sworn testimony of his brother.

Will Sheppard seemed half asleep. He had paid no attention to the prosecuting attorney while he pointed out the various sections of land Bob Rutledge claimed. Shep's thoughts seemed far away.

When it came his turn to question Tracy Banning, he got slowly to his feet and walked over as close as he could stand to the witness box.

'Is it, or is it not, true that the feud between the Bannings and the Rutledges carries back to the third generation, to the time when a Banning rebel refused to surrender and fled to Texas, and fought a gun duel with a Rutledge, a survivor of Quantrill's Guerrillas? Answer the question "yes" or "no".'

'Yes,' came Tracy Banning's reluctant reply, 'but what has that got to do with Bob Rutledge stealing all the land he can get hold of?'

'The answer was "yes." I move that the rest of Tracy Banning's addition to the answer be stricken from the court records.'

'Objection sustained. Strike the rest out,' said the judge, wide awake now for the first time in hours.

'Did, or did not, those men fight the gun duel over a little Mexican dance-hall girl neither of them ever saw before or afterwards? Answer "yes" or "no".'

'Yes,' snapped Tracy Banning, red faced, 'but let me tell you something right now. The Bannings come from a breed that never forgets nor forgives a grudge. The feud was passed down to the Banning sons. My brother Taylor and myself are the last of the Banning men and the feud between us and the last of the Rutledge clan is still alive and all the more bitter for the Banning blood that has been spilled.'

Will Sheppard bowed. He looked up at the judge. 'If it pleases Your Honour, the defence allows the added testimony of the witness to stand.'

The young prosecutor was on his feet, red faced with suppressed anger. 'I move that the added testimony be stricken from the records of the court, on the basis that it is irrelevant and immaterial and has nothing to do with the case of land fraud involved.'

'Your Honour,' Will Sheppard was on his feet and his voice cut like a whetted blade through his opponent's bluster, 'I will prove, before this case goes to the jury room, that Tracy Banning's added testimony is relevant, material and vital in the summing-up of the testimony for the defence.

'Allow me, Your Honour, and Gentlemen of the Jury, to add a few words explaining my reasons. You have heard the witness, Tracy Banning, state under oath that the bitter, blood-spattered feud between the Bannings and the Rutledges had its beginning in a gun duel over a woman.' Shep touched the red carnation and when he looked into Georgia Banning's unflinching eyes he smiled faintly.

'Before the defence closes I will prove beyond all doubt that there is a woman involved in the feud the Bannings have built up against their neighbour Robert Rutledge and his son Brad. The lady involved is the daughter of Taylor Banning. No finer or braver lady than Georgia Banning ever lived. She is here in this court room of her own free will, despite the protests of her father and uncle.

'I will try to lift Georgia Banning and her splendid courage beyond the touch of bloodstains shed by brave men on both the Banning and Rutledge sides. All those men died bravely and according to their lights because of an unknown woman that two men shed their death's blood to stain the soil of Texas. I will strive to do the best I know how to answer the prayer in the heart of Georgia Banning that no more Banning and Rutledge blood will spill on the ground of Montana.'

Will Sheppard's face had paled from the inner efforts of his own pleading. He stifled a cough with the clean white linen handkerchief he placed quickly over his mouth. When he took it away the handkerchief was crimson stained, which the judge and the jurymen could not help but see.

'I apologize to the court for this unseeming burst of oratory.' As Shep took his seat his eyes met those of Georgia Banning. She smiled faintly and nodded.

Tracy Banning was livid. But there was a secret smile on Taylor Banning's hard-lipped mouth. His hand found that of his daughter. There were unshed tears in her eyes when she looked up at him and smiled.

Shep filled the tumbler full of the colourless liquid and gulped it down like a thirsty man drinking water. He leaned back exhausted, closing his eyes, relaxing.

The eyes of Brad Rutledge and Georgia Banning met and held for a brief moment. Bob Rutledge sat hunched in his big armchair. His bushy brows knitted in a scowl as he glared at Tracy Banning. Chalk tugged gently at the handcuffs.

'Mistah Shep,' Chalk whispered huskily, 'he ain't long

for this world.' Chalk's hoarse whisper carried to the front row behind the low railing.

'Proceed,' the voice of the grey-haired judge sounded across the court room.

The prosecuting attorney got slowly to his feet. Something of his cocksure attitude had wilted.

'Your Honour, I move that further testimony in the case be postponed until tomorrow morning.'

The judge looked up at the clock. The hands stood at two-thirty in the afternoon.

'Motion denied. Any more witnesses?'

'The prosecution has no more witnesses.'

'Any witnesses for the defence.'

Will Sheppard rose to his feet, with a seeming visible effort, and rested his weight against the table.

'The defence has no witnesses, Your Honour.'

'Then get on with your rebuttal, Mr. Prosecutor.'

Reluctantly the young prosecutor took up his long pointer and moved towards the map.

'I will not take up your time, Your Honour, and Gentlemen of the Jury. I have already made it as plain as I possibly can that the accused, Robert Rutledge, is guilty beyond all doubt of fraudulent land grabbing.

'My worthy opponent has resorted to cheap trickery to work up sympathy for a man who is guilty of grand theft. Will Sheppard is an accomplished actor. 'A charlatan with a prison record. He must resort to cheap trickery to win the sympathy of the court. To blind you gentlemen of the jury with a skilful blindfold so that your sympathies might be swayed. This land-grabbing case has nothing to do with the feud between the Bannings and the Rutledges.

'I charge you twelve gentlemen of the jury,' the prosecuting attorney gripped the wooden rail of the jury box with both hands, his voice vibrant with emotion, 'to do your sworn duty. The defendant is guilty . . . Guilty!' He pounded the rail with both clenched fists.

'Are you going to be swayed from the straight path of your duty as jurymen? Are you going to be led far afield by the inebriated dramatic antics of Will Sheppard?'

The over-zealous young prosecutor turned abruptly. He

walked with long strides towards the table where the
defence attorney slumped, his eyes half-lidded, his face
drawn and pale-looking. He picked up the pitcher from which
Shep had been drinking and carried it back to the jury rail.
He shoved it into the hands of the foreman of the jury.

'Smell what little is left in this pitcher,' he told the jury
foreman, 'then pass it along.'

The jury foreman sniffed, then passed it to the next man.
The young prosecutor waited until it had gone the rounds,
then handed the pitcher to the judge. The judge smelled it and
set it down alongside the papers in front of him.

The young prosecutor pointed an accusing finger at Shep,
who sprawled in the chair.

'That man is drunk! It is a disgrace and a mockery of justice to have a drunken attorney-at-law turn a court room into
a cheap vaudeville house for his maudlin clowning!' He
paused, paled by the intensity of his emotions.

'I move that the jury retire before they are forced to listen
to further irrelevant babbling by my drunken opponent.'

The judge rapped for order in the court as the crowd
stirred and muttered.

'Motion denied,' said the judge. 'Another such outburst
will find you in contempt of court. Confine your oratorical
abilities to the material and relevant facts. You may proceed with your rebuttal.'

The young attorney, reddened with rebuke, walked back
to the jury box. He made a gesture of resigned helplessness.

'Robert Rutledge is guilty, Gentlemen of the Jury. It is your
duty to find him guilty of grand theft. I have nothing more
to say. Except to thank you for your patience with the va-
garies of this court.' He sat down beside Ike Markson, whose
oily face had a worried look.

It seemed to tax all of Will Sheppard's strength to lift himself from his chair. His face looked drawn and white as
he walked slowly towards the jury box. He took a wallet
from the inside pocket of his coat and opened it, taking out
a slip of paper. He handed it to the foreman of the jury to
read. Then he walked slowly over to the judge's stand, and
handed him the paper.

'I would deem it a favour, Your Honour, if you would read

it aloud. My young opponent has branded me in this court as a maudlin drunkard, which is a blot of dishonour on my name.'

The judge read aloud. 'Will Sheppard is my patient and as his doctor I have prescribed alcoholic stimulant. It is vital to my patient's health and well-being, especially while he is under mental and physical strain in the court room. I have prescribed one quart of gin tonic per day while the court is in session. Signed John Steele, M.D.'

The judge docketed the slip on his steel file and handed the pitcher to Will Sheppard.

'Thank you, Your Honour.' Shep put the pitcher back on the table and picked up the rawhide reata and walked over to the jury box. Still holding the rope in his hands, he addressed both the judge and the jury.

'My young and able opponent has proved, beyond all shadow of doubt, the guilt of my old friend and client. Your Honour, Gentlemen of the Jury, I wish to enter, in behalf of Robert Rutledge, a plea of Guilty. Robert Rutledge throws himself upon the mercy, that should temper justice, of this court.'

'Your plea of Guilty is entered in this court,' said the judge. 'Proceed.'

'I have here in my hands,' Shep spoke quietly, 'the rope that was used as a fifty-foot surveyor's chain to measure the land Bob Rutledge claimed according to the law of metes and bounds.' Shep looked at the reata and smiled faintly. The smile still on his face, he looked up at the twelve men in the jury box. He made his formal salutation to the judge, then began his final address to the jury. He turned slowly to take in the entire court room.

'Gentlemen, the day of the open range is gone. The land that was measured off with this reata was free range that must be divided by the laws of progress. Men like Bob Rutledge must move on, on to other frontiers, there to make safe the coming of those who plough up the pioneer trails. I ask nothing of you gentlemen but your understanding of this man who is on trial. Were it not for men like Bob Rutledge, frontiers would never be crossed. I have called no witnesses in this case. Bob Rutledge came to Montana to live

97

in peace. He left Texas and the Banning-Rutledge feud. But Taylor and Tracy Banning followed him from Texas as soon as they found out he was building up a cattle empire in Montana. They were not willing to let the feud die. They came here to wipe out the last of the Rutledges.'

The drop of a pin could be heard in the court room. Everyone listened and was tense while Will Sheppard talked of feuds and hardships, and enmities. He spoke of long days in the saddle, long nights of travel from Texas to Montana. He bared the life of Bob Rutledge and cited him as the bravest man he had ever known. He told of Brad as a small boy being taken from one frontier to the next, cow country, mining camps, mountains where the snow drifted across their blankets, the desert with its sun and thirst. He spoke of death. He spoke of senseless, useless range feuds, the futile shedding of brave blood.

Never before had judge or jury or court room audience listened to such eloquence.

'Gentlemen, it is not the men who handle the guns and kill each other wantonly who suffer most. It is the grief-burdened women they leave behind who bear the brunt of brutal killing. In this case it will be Georgia Banning and Brad Rutledge. I helped raise Brad from boyhood. For many long years I taught him the folly of carrying a gun, and until a few weeks ago Brad Rutledge never owned a gun of any kind. It was only when his life was threatened that I urged the boy I love like a son to carry a gun. I would not have him shot down, unarmed and unable to defend his life, by a hired killer.

'Your Honour, Gentlemen of the Jury, my client Robert Rutledge is eager and willing to pay for all the State and Government lands that he has surveyed and claimed.

'Bob Rutledge is past the prime of life. Shut him in a prison cell and he will die quickly in confinement. That will mean Brad Rutledge, if the young man escapes a cowardly assassin's bullet, will inherit the Block R outfit.'

Shep walked over to where Brad sat handcuffed to Chalk. He took the red carnation from his buttonhole and ran it through the buttonhole of Brad's blue flannel shirt.

'Unlock the handcuffs,' Shep whispered in Brad's ear as he

bent over. 'Be ready to get on your feet when I tell you.'

Will Sheppard walked back in front of the judge's stand. He looked at Georgia Banning.

'Miss Georgia, I have no wish to further embarrass you in this court . . .'

Before Shep could finish, Georgia Banning got to her feet. She shook off the hand that her Uncle Tracy had put on her arm. Head held high, she spoke in a clear voice.

'What is it, Shep?' she asked.

'If you were free to decide,' Will Sheppard put his question slowly, 'would you fulfil the promise you made in my cabin one night, to marry Brad Rutledge?'

Shep quickly signalled Brad to his feet.

'I am willing to marry Brad Rutledge,' Georgia Banning was looking at Brad, 'any place, and at any time.'

'On behalf of Brad and speaking for myself, I thank you for your courageous reply. That is all.'

Still holding the rawhide reata in his hands, Shep looked at it silently, musingly for a short moment.

'Gentlemen, the law of the rope passed when the Vigilantes of Montana disbanded. The man who takes the law into his hands and shoots another man because of some remote ancestral grudge is guilty of murder.'

Shep put the rope on the judge's desk.

'I place this rawhide reata and the cattleman to whom it belongs at the mercy of Your Honour and the twelve men and true who comprise the jury.'

Will Sheppard looked drawn and white with exhaustion. Emotion strained his face. He choked up on the last words and was seized by a coughing spell that racked his spare frame. Before his trembling hand could get the handkerchief from his pocket, a crimson froth showed at the corners of his mouth. He stood there swaying.

Brad reached Shep's side in time to catch the attorney as his knees buckled. He walked him slowly to his chair and eased him into it.

A funereal hush fell across the court room. The spectators who had come here anticipating excitement and drama were getting their fill of it. The judge cleared his throat, and spoke in a sonorous voice.

99

'The accused, Robert Rutledge, will rise to his feet while the sentence of this court of justice is pronounced. Inasmuch as the attorney for the defence has changed his plea to Guilty, it will not be necessary for the jurymen to leave their seats.'

Bob Rutledge got slowly to his feet and stood there, high-headed, cold-eyed.

The judge spoke. 'After due consideration, knowing all the facts of the case and the circumstances behind it, Robert Rutledge is found Guilty. Therefore, I sentence him to the maximum limit of twenty-five years in the Montana State prison!'

Bob Rutledge stiffened, but his eyes never flinched as he met the eyes of the judge.

The young prosecutor, flushed by an unexpected victory, looked at the two Bannings, and smiled. Georgia's face was pale, her eyes dark with pity.

The judge went on. 'Furthermore, this court fines the accused the maximum fine of five thousand dollars!'

A low, ominous murmur swept the packed room. The judge rapped for order.

'Have you anything to say for yourself, Robert Rutledge?'

'I have nothing to say, Your Honour.' Bob Rutledge spoke in a clear voice.

The judge's words again fell across the tense silence.

'This court suspends the prison sentence, and remits the fine, all but a nominal grazing fee for the State and Government lands, the amount to be fixed later by the land appraisers.

'This court has strived to temper justice with mercy and therefore balance the scales. I trust the findings of this court meet with your approval.'

The jury foreman was on his feet. 'On behalf of the jury, I wish to congratulate Your Honour on his decision.'

'Clear the court room!' The judge's wooden gavel was pounding. The sound was drowned out by the cheers of the crowd.

Georgia Banning had gone up to Brad. Brad took her in his arms, holding her close, and kissed her.

Taylor Banning, backed by Tracy, shouldered his way

100

through the crowd to get his daughter. He grabbed her arm and with him and Tracy on either side of her they got her out of the court room by way of the back door a deputy held open.

Shep and Bob Rutledge shook hands with the judge and each of the twelve men of the jury. They left the court room and boarded the train for home.

Later, inside Shep's cabin, with Brad and Chalk there, out on bail bond furnished by Bob Rutledge, Shep smiled his twisted smile and quirked an eyebrow at Brad. He took something from his breast pocket and tossed it on the table. It was the flattened .45 slug that had almost cost Brad his life.

'I wasn't coughing up a lung, there in the court room,' Shep said quietly. 'Before court went into session I had the dentist pull a wisdom tooth. At the crucial moment I faked the cough and slipped that lead slug into my mouth. Tongued it back into the cavity and bit down hard to start the bleeding.'

Shep opened his brief case and took from it the rawhide reata and hung it on a wooden peg over the fireplace. Then he filled his glass and the glass of Bob Rutledge to the brim with twenty-year-old rye whisky.

'That rope came damn near hanging you, Robert,' said Shep, 'but for the splendid courage of a lady named Georgia Banning.'

'Here's to the smartest damn lawyer alive.' Bob Rutledge raised his glass and drank.

'Abilene Adams,' said Shep, 'and Joe Slocum were conspicious at the trial, by their absence.'

'I gave Ab orders to stay at the ranch,' said Bob Rutledge. 'I expect the Bannings gave Joe Slocum the same orders.'

'But I'm ready to lay odds that neither of those men are there now,' said Shep. 'They're making war medicine somewhere in the badlands. They're waiting for the warm Chinook spring wind to melt the drifts. If the Bannings and the Rutledges fail to kill each other off, down to the last men, Abilene Adams and Joe Slocum are preparing to do some killing. They're willing to take abuse from the Block R and the BB owners during the long winter months. When the country is laid bare, they will strike and strike hard. Abilene has always hated Brad's guts and now he's turned on you, Robert. He has two bullets marked Rutledge. Joe Slocum will kill the Banning brothers, saving Georgia. There is a cattle empire at stake. And Abilene Adams and Joe Slocum are high stake gamblers.'

Chalk grinned as he went about getting supper. In Chalk's book, Shep was the smartest man in the world, bar none. After supper, Brad cleared the table and piled the dishes in the sink for Shep's squaw housekeeper who came in the early morning. They sat around and smoked while Chalk played his old battered banjo and sang.

They all knew it was to be their last night together for a while, but nobody mentioned it. Bob Rutledge was taking Shep to the home ranch. Brad and Chalk, out on bond, were headed for Brad's place down on the river. At daybreak they would pull out, ride together as far as the Block R home ranch. From there, Brad and Chalk would go on.

But tonight, sitting beside an open fire in Shep's cabin, nobody made mention of the dangerous days and weeks and months of winter that lay ahead. Months of below zero weather and hardships and empty bellies, while they waited for the Chinook wind to melt the snowdrifts and break apart the deep winter ice of the wide Missouri river, when the inevitable range war would break into gunfire.

Despite Will Sheppard's plea in court, Bob Rutledge and his son would be packing guns. Tracy and Taylor Banning would ride together heavily armed. And every cowhand working for the Block R and BB outfits would ride in pairs and be ready to shoot.

'Do the Bannings know about Ab Adams and Joe Slocum throwing in together?' Bob Rutledge put the question to Shep while Chalk took time off for a smoke.

'I told Georgia Banning to warn her father that Joe Slocum had formed a dangerous alliance with Abilene Adams, but they're apt to discount what I say,' said Shep.

They pulled out at daybreak. The barn man told them that the Bannings had pulled out not more than a half-hour ahead. They had Georgia with them.

Shep gave the grizzled barn man a drink out of his bottle.

'Miss Georgia leave any word of any kind?' Shep asked.

'Only a played-out old red flower she said to give to Brad Rutledge.'

Brad's face reddened. He grinned faintly.

'I wouldn't try to get in touch with her,' Shep said in a low tone as they got ready to start. 'I gave Georgia the same warning. It might precipitate matters, and do no good except to cause trouble. You got a bond of love to hold you until the proper time comes. You both leave it to Shep.'

'All right, Shep . . . but it's going to be tough separated.' Brad suddenly remembered the woman Shep had loved and lost. It made him feel like a whiner.

CHAPTER XVI

ABILENE ADAMS was waiting there at the Block R ranch when they pulled in. He looked them over, bleak-eyed.

'How'd you come out at the trial, Bob?' he asked.

'The judge threw the book at me, Ab,' Bob Rutledge grinned. 'Then he turned around and got big-hearted. Looks like I'm on a kind of probation from here on. Shep got me off lucky.'

'I thought you had tied the can to Shep? What became of Ike Markson?'

'Ike Markson went over to the Bannings, where he belongs. Last I seen of him he was taking the train back to Butte.' Bob Rutledge was in rare good humour and in an expansive mood. A twinkle showed in his hard eyes when he spoke again.

'If ever you take a notion to kill that BB ramrod, Joe Slocum,' he chuckled, 'Shep's the man can get you off.'

Adam's pale eyes narrowed as he cut a suspicious look at the four men.

'Every now and then,' Ab Adams measured his words as if he had rehearsed what he had to say, 'I run into Joe Slocum in my travels. Like as not we've been seen together. Seems

103

like Joe Slocum is feeling me out, to see where I stand with the Block R outfit. I've been leading him on, sorta. Letting on like I was willing to throw in with him if the jackpot was big enough.'

Ab Adams paused to light the cigarette he had rolled. His eyes were wary as he looked up at Brad.

'Seems like Joe Slocum wants to kill you off, Brad, on account of Georgia Banning. Slocum claims him and Georgia were all set to get married. Then you fished her out of the creek and from what Joe tells me you still got the girl on the end of your rope.'

Brad Rutledge was fighting to keep his temper under control. He knew Adams was baiting him, ribbing him into some kind of quarrel. He caught the warning look in Shep's eyes and that helped him play it easy. Brad's jaws were clamped till the muscles bunched and quivered.

'Did Joe Slocum divulge any of his plans for the near future, Abilene?' asked Shep.

'Not too much.' Ab Adams was playing it close to his belly. 'I ain't got that far into his confidence. But I know this much. Joe had a run-in with Taylor Banning on account of his daughter, but her Uncle Tracy is all for her marrying Joe. And Slocum ain't the man to give up easy. He's got his eye on the BB outfit. When the two Bannings die, the ranch goes to Georgia Banning. Joe Slocum aims to marry the BB outfit."

Abilene Adams let on as if he was telling some great secret, instead of peddling what was common range gossip. He was fooling nobody, not even himself, perhaps.

'Where do you come into the deal, Abilene?' asked Shep with a deceptive mildness.

'I was coming to that,' said Adams. 'All Joe Slocum has been doing so far is throwing out fellers. He even accused me of playing both ends against the middle, and he sure hit the nail on the head. But I managed to talk him out of that notion. After we had killed a quart between us, he began feeling me out. He said that Bob Rutledge was bound to go to the pen, and that would leave Brad in charge of the Block R. He bragged how he'll kill you, Brad, and he told me to kill Chalk. That would leave me ramrodding the Block R,

104

and he'd be owner, him and his wife, of the BB outfit. We'd throw the two outfits together and we'd be sitting on top of the Montana cow country for a world. Joe Slocum made it sound like shore sweet music.' Ab Adams relit his half-smoked cigarette.

'Chalk here,' Shep spoke quietly, 'plays the sweetest music any man ever wanted to hear. But he could throw a sour note into that sweet duet the pair of you are now collaborating on. You might pass that on to Cousin Joe Slocum for what it's worth next time you hold a rendezvous in the badlands, Abilene.'

'You never did put any trust in me, Shep,' Ab Adams said, 'and that goes double, mister. You and your damned shyster talk.' Adams turned his back to Shep to speak to Bob Rutledge.

'I've killed my share of the Banning tribe, Bob, before we ever met up with this whisky-head Shep. I want to know where I stand with you.'

'You stand on your own legs, Ab,' Bob Rutledge said quietly, 'and you'll stand all right with the Block R, and you always will until you prove otherwise.'

'I'm playing a dangerous game with Joe Slocum. I've gone this far with it. I'm willing to go farther. But I've got to have a free rein.'

'You'll get it, Ab,' said Bob Rutledge. 'Throw in with Joe Slocum if you want to play it that away. But I'm warning you now, Ab, if you travel his gait too far, you'll pull up lame.'

'That'll be my risk,' Ab Adams said grimly. He headed for the bunkhouse. Nobody spoke till he went inside and closed the door behind him.

Shep answered the question in Bob Rutledge's eyes.

'The usually taciturn Abilene could be on the level, Robert. But I can't help but wonder what prompted the always silent Abilene to burst forth in so much voluble oratory. That goes on record in my book as the longest speech he ever made in his life. There's too much smoke for a tiny blaze. I needled him deliberately, but he told us nothing we do not already know. I'm willing to lay odds that it was Joe Slocum's idea that prompted this seemingly frank outburst. This business of pulling the wool across our eyes. It was Abilene Adams who hired Markson to feel Brad out about selling the KC ranch, after Adams and Joe Slocum threw in together to kill off the Bannings and the Rutledges and claim everything. Chalk kept a pretty close check on those two when he first went down into the badlands to hide out, and he says their meetings were frequent.

'As it happens, it has only strengthened my first suspicions of the treachery of Abilene Adams and his growing hatred for Brad.

'It's time you and Chalk changed horses and pulled out. As it is it will be long past dark when you get to the KC ranch,' Shep told Brad.

When they had changed to fresh horses, Bob Rutledge gripped Brad's hand.

'Take care of yourself, son. When the time comes I'll be there at your wedding.'

Brad knew that it cost his father a lot in the way of pride to make that statement. But before he could find the words, Bob Rutledge was headed for the bunkhouse.

"Stay at your ranch, Brad,' Shep said. 'Ride herd on the boy, Chalk.'

Shep shoved a letter into Brad's hand. 'That's a note from the sheriff. You hand it to his deputy in charge of the two cowhands who are feeding your hay to a lot of cattle. We'll send the Banning brothers a feed bill after the Chinook. So-long and good luck.'

CHAPTER XVII

It must have been sometime around midnight when Chalk and Brad neared the KC ranch on the Missouri river. It was a clear, cold January night and the stars had a cold white sparkle and the moon was full and bright.

From the high ridge the log buildings and pole corrals of

the ranch below stood out against the white snow. Great bare patches showed where the snowplough had cleared strips between the cattleshed and the river where the hay had been scattered each day to feed the weaker cattle, and on that bare ground hundreds of cattle were bedded down for the night.

It all made for a peaceful setting there in the moonlight, but it was a deceptive sort of serenity. Brad and Chalk watched for any sign of lurking danger that might be waiting for them.

They were plain targets as they rode down the slope and across the bottom lands. Brad leaned from his saddle to pull the wooden gate pin. He swung the gate open and they rode through. When Brad shoved the pin back to close the gate, Chalk was already fifty yards away. His saddle gun was across his saddle and his fur mittens dangled from leather cords. Chalk had levered a shell from the magazine into the breech of the gun and his finger was on the trigger.

Brad lifted his horse to a trot to overtake Chalk.

'That'll be far enough!' barked a voice from the dark interior of the barn. 'Stand your hand! What fetches you here?'

'Who wants to know?' Brad called back.

'The law!' came the reply.

'Step out Mistah Law,' Chalk called. 'It's only Brad Rutledge and ol' Chalk.'

A short, heavy-set man in a big buffalo coat stepped out of the dark barn. He had a saddle carbine in his hands.

'I'm here alone,' said the deputy sheriff. 'I've been waiting for the sheriff to send somebody down to take my place. I'm short-handed. One of my men got killed and the other scared off. I'd have bunched it myself if I didn't have this hellslue of cattle to feed and water. I've been sleeping in the barn for three nights. Them bushwhackers shot the windowpanes out of the cabin. I sent the dead man's body to town with the man who quit.'

'How long has this been going on?' asked Brad.

'For about a week. One of my men was shot in the back night before last, the other pulled out yesterday. He got the idea it was you and Chalk doing the shooting, knowing you were on the dodge, but I didn't see eye to eye with him.

107

There were always two riders, but it was hard to identify them all bundled up for the winter, and they never came that close, anyhow.

'I don't know for certain if they killed my man a-purpose, or not. It looked like they was just trying to spook the three of us and keep us boogered, in the hopes we'd leave. They must have had their gun sights raised to the last notch, they kept that far away.'

'When did they show last time?'

'Last night.'

'Me and Chalk have alibis for the last three nights. Two of them we spent in town and last night at the Block R ranch. We're out on heavy bail bond right now. We're going to spend the rest of the winter down here. I got a letter from the sheriff to give to you. You can stay or you can pull out for town. Make it easy on yourself.'

'I'm pulling out at daybreak,' said the deputy, 'but you better get some help. There's twice the cattle across the river as there is on this side. Hay to scatter for them that can't rustle for feed in the breaks. Waterholes to chop open twice a day. We took turns at first going over across the river. Then my two men balked and wouldn't cross the river, and I found out why. About the time they laid their guns aside for axes to chop holes in the ice, or were on top of a load of hay with pitchforks in their hands, a 30-30 bullet would whine so close they'd have to duck. They were shooting to miss, but when that keeps up day after day and of a night, a man gets jumpy. You'll find out for yourselves. I've done quit.'

'Don't know as I can blame you,' said Brad.

They slipped their beds off the pack-horses at the cabin, then stabled their saddle-horses and pack-horses in the barn.

While Brad spread their beds on the empty bunks, Chalk made coffee and cooked steaks and hot biscuits.

The deputy read the sheriff's letter in grim silence. He looked up with a faint grin on his whiskered, frostbitten face.

'The sheriff says here that John Law is pulling out of the game. Let the Bannings and the Rutledges fight it out.'

Brad looked surprised. He had figured he and Chalk would be more or less in the protective custody of the law. But

108

Chalk nodded and grinned as he poured steaming black coffee into the big tin cups.

'Mistah Shep,' he mused aloud, 'smartest man on earth.' Chalk had no use for man-made laws nor the peace officers who enforced those laws.

In a way Brad felt relieved not to be under the watchful and wary and somewhat distrustful eye of some man wearing a law badge. He knew neither he nor Chalk would make any deliberate move to violate the terms of their heavy bail. But it might turn out that they would be crowded into a gunplay, regardless. And neither of them wanted to be under a restraining hand. They'd shoot and shoot first and shoot to kill, if it came to a showdown.

This move was contrary to all that Shep had said when he made his plea in court, knowing his every word was spoken tongue-in-cheek. Men born and reared according to feud rule knew no other law than the law of their own guns. It was bred both in the Bannings and the Rutledges, even Brad and Georgia felt the taint of it in their blood.

With Brad and Chalk at the ranch, the deputy felt almost secure. Both men showed a sort of callous indifference to any danger. Chalk cussed the shots that had busted the windowpanes to let the cold air into the cabin. He nailed a double thickness of heavy canvas across the two windows, and said he would board the windows up next day.

Brad asked the deputy if he had a tally on the cattle that were being wintered at the KC place. But nobody had taken the trouble to get a count on the cattle that drifted in from the badlands.

'All I know is that there's too many cattle for you two men to take care of without three-four men to help you.'

'We'll manage,' said Brad. 'You been doing any "rawhiding" back in the breaks?'

"Hell, no. We ain't set foot off the place. Bad enough being shot at here where a man can duck behind something. I wouldn't ride into the breaks to make myself a pot-shot target. I'm turning in this tin badge when I get to town. I got a warm job tending bar awaiting me.'

They were glad to see the law officer pull out after breakfast. After he had gone, Brad and Chalk got a tally on the cattle that fed and watered on both sides of the river.

'We'll be lucky if the hay holds out, Chalk. Looks like we're feeding half the cattle in the Block R and BB irons. There's a lot of those big native steers should be cut out and shoved into the breaks. They don't need hay. Those three scared-to-death men have been wasting good hay. A lot of those steers are fat enough to butcher for beef.'

'Cabin fever,' grinned Chalk. 'Those three fellers were took down bad with cabin fever. Shovelling hay and chopping waterholes and holing-up in a warm cabin come early dark. A small boy with a lightin' bug fastened to a corncob could run all three of them out of the country. They sho'. put a big dent in our winter grub. Me'n you'll be eating straight beef before spring.'

Brad and Chalk were up long before daylight, scattering hay and chopping waterholes. Every day they rode into the breaks and brought in the weak cattle that needed feeding. Early breakfast and late supper and no meal in between.

Now and then they sighted riders in the distance. Always in pairs and beyond rifle range. They never came close enough now to do any shooting. They must have known that the deputies had gone and that Chalk and Brad were now in charge.

They kept the pole gate padlocked. Chalk had found a dozen or more horse bells and several strings of sleigh bells in the barn. He wired each bell to the barbed wire fence, stringing them out for half a mile, to give the alarm should any night riders be tempted to cut the fence and ride through.

Several times during the following weeks Chalk and Brad would come awake when a bell would sound. Dressed and outside with their saddle carbines. But it was always cattle walking the fence that set off the alarm. And Chalk and Brad would be cramped and shivering with cold when they got back to the cabin.

Every two or three weeks a Block R cowman would show up, to see how they were making it. He brought mail and a sack full of newspapers and periodicals. Always there would be a short note from Bob Rutledge or a longer note from Shep.

Everything was going all right at the home ranch. There was no news of any startling importance.

110

'I could be mistaken concerning the amiable Abilene,' wrote Shep. 'Each week there is a gold star on his report card. Even when the genial Abilene plays hooky he shows valid excuse for his absence.'

Each time Brad opened the mail sack he hoped there would be a letter from Georgia Banning. And every time he was doomed to the same bitter disappointment.

Brad was tempted to write to her. But always he decided against it. In the first place he felt certain that the letter would never reach her. Anything he might say in a letter would only complicate an already difficult position for her.

As Chalk tried to explain it to Brad. He and Georgia knew all that there was to know about the bond of love between them. Putting words on paper to express what they both felt would only make the long waiting seem longer. It would gain neither of them anything but impatience. Brad didn't see eye to eye with Chalk's reasoning. What if her father and her uncle were talking her out of the notion of marrying a Rutledge? Talking her into marrying her Cousin Joe? Poisoning her mind against Brad with clever lies?

Chalk shook his head and said that any girl who had the courage to stand up that day in court and declare herself, it would take more than talk to change her mind.

To Chalk's way of thinking, all women were troublesome. If a man was fool enough to take them serious. Even honkeytonk girls were worrisome. A man had to watch himself or he'd get cut up or shot.

Chalk had had his share of women all his life, and figured on having more than his share as time went on, but he took them all in his giant stride. With a chuckle or a laugh, and afterwards a song to remember each one of them by. Chalk had always been carefree to hear him tell it.

But Shep had told Brad a different story, and Chalk had old knife scars and a couple of small puckered bullet holes in his hide to prove otherwise.

'Shep tells it different,' Brad would put in after Chalk had given him a lot of fatherly advice. 'According to Shep, Chalk used to be Muy Hombre, much man, along the border.'

Chalk's eyes would roll with his white-tooth grin and he

would dance the double shuffle on the hard-packed dirt floor of the cabin.

'Ol' Chalk was just funnin',' Chalk would pass it off when he would relate some knife or gun fight over a woman. 'Just funnin'.'

Brad and Chalk were holed-up in a snowed-in cabin for the second time that winter. The short days and the long lonesome nights were a rigid test of their ability to stand up under the strain.

Chalk played his banjo and made up a new song about a white mule that learned to talk, and the circuit rider preacher who rode the mule from one camp meeting to the next. Never the same story twice, because Chalk had a fertile brain. But always the white mule would talk at the most embarrassing times and in the wrong places. The way Chalk would fit the words to the tune was enough to drive away the blues. Chalk could make his old banjo bray like a mule.

Sometimes in the dead of night the river ice would pop, loud as any cannon. They would both come awake, their guns in their hands. Other nights there would be the whine of the north wind driving the hard, dry snow against the cabin walls and the boarded-up windows. When it swept around the corners of the cabin it sounded for all the world like men whispering outside. They would both lie awake in spite of their better judgment, gripping their guns.

Or there would be the yapping of coyotes on the night prowl. Or the lonely howl of a wolf back in the badlands. Or the woman-like scream of a mountain lion that chilled a man's spine and tightened his scalp. Brad never got used to the night scream of a mountain lion.

And day or night there was the constant sense of lurking danger that kept a man's nerves on edge. The fear of a bushwhacker's bullet.

Brad and Chalk knew, even as the Banning brothers and Bob Rutledge knew, likewise Ab Adams and Joe Slocum were aware of the fact, and Will Sheppard was counting on it, that so long as the winter was holding them all in its snowbound grip there would be no open war declared.

It was a full-time job for all the cowhands working for the Block R and BB outfits, in the saddle from daybreak till

112

dark, to handle the cattle. Winter is no time to declare open season in a gun feud. Twenty, thirty, sometimes forty below zero is no kind of weather to go gunning. The bitter cold would cramp a man's gun hand, stiffen his frostbitten fingers. A man all bundled up in fleecelined underwear and heavy pants and wool shirt and bulky overcoat, chaps and four-buckled overshoes, earflaps tied down, is certainly in no shape to make a fast gun-play.

Even for the cold-blooded, murder-minded bushwhacker, there is the snow to leave the tell-tale tracks from the scene of the murder to camp or ranch.

Therefore, the feud between the Bannings and the Rutledges was frozen in for the winter.

Save for the annoying tactics of the two night riders who had annoyed the three deputies sent down to take over the KC ranch. Chalk was inclined to lay it to those two quick-triggered gents' hatred for a law badge. It irked both sides of the feuding factions for the law to be dealt in. Brad was inclined to think along the same line of thought expressed by Chalk.

Brad, however, held back certain reservations. There was a strong taint of personal enmity to it. If the men were Abilene Adams and Joe Slocum, and there was every reason to pin it down to those two renegades, both men had plenty of cause to hate Brad, and they wanted the KC ranch.

'Figure it this way, Chalk,' Brad said. 'If Ab Adams and Joe Slocum had run those three men off, they could have moved in. When it's all said and done, possession is nine-tenths of the law. Once moved in, they would have been hard to smoke out. They had every reason to believe that Bob Rutledge would be sent to the pen. They were waiting for the news. It must have given Ab Adams a jolt when my father showed up at the home ranch.'

Chalk and Brad both agreed that if Bob Rutledge had been sent to the pen, Adams and Slocum would have moved in and held the KC outfit, in spite of hell and snowdrifts and blizzards, till the Chinook wind cut the drifts. They figured Brad and Chalk were on the dodge from the law and wouldn't cause them any trouble.

113

It stood to reason that was the game of freeze-out Ab Adams and Joe Slocum were playing.

'And it wouldn't surprise me none,' said Brad, 'if Tracy Banning had a hand in the deal.'

'Could be,' nodded Chalk, 'could be.'

'But Shep threw a monkeywrench into the works by freeing my father and getting us out on bail bond.'

That got a chuckle out of Chalk. 'Mistah Shep, he smart.'

So they all waited for the coming of spring and the warm Chinook wind.

There was a calendar on the wall and Brad marked off each day when they came into the cabin at night. The month of February was torn off and it was well into the month of March when Shep's letter came with a short note from Bob Rutledge. A Block R cowhand brought the mail, stayed overnight, then went back to the home ranch.

The note from Bob Rutledge, who hated to write letters, was short and told them nothing, except that rheumatism has got into his joints. For Brad and Chalk to take care of themselves and he'd be seeing them soon.

Shep's note was short in length, but pithy in its contents. 'With the first warnings of the Chinook, I will send word to Taylor and Tracy Banning to bring along what cowhands they need to move their cattle from your KC ranch on to their own range. Bob Rutledge and Abilene will take the Block R crew and move down to the KC place. Both the BB and the Block R outfit will have to pay you, Brad, either in cash or by certified cheque, before any cattle are moved.

'I have taken the necessary steps, according to the laws of Montana, to have the cattle impounded at the KC ranch, to be held there, ten days after said Notice of Impoundment is posted publicly and printed in the local newspapers, said notice to run for ten consecutive issues of the newspapers. If at the end of ten days the necessary cash or certified cheque for the full amount is not posted, all cattle in any brands whatsoever that you have wintered belong to you, to be sold at sheriff's sale at public auction, there at the KC ranch.

'I am sending you this advance notice so that you and Chalk will be duly prepared and forewarned.

'I will be there as sole representative of the law when the BB and Block R outfits move in. Wait for me before you allow them to take over.'

There was no word of any kind concerning Georgia Banning.

But among the roll of newspapers Brad found a marked copy of the *Enterprise*. He read it and re-read it till his eyes blurred.

'It is rumoured that wedding bells will ring in the month of June, for Miss Georgia Banning, daughter of Taylor Banning. The lucky man is Joe Slocum, foreman and ramrod for the Banning BB outfit.'

Brad balled the newspaper and shoved it into the little sheet-iron stove, without reading it aloud, as was his wont, to Chalk.

CHAPTER XVIII

THE long awaited Chinook wind came in the middle of the night. Both Brad and Chalk awoke to the soft whine of it and both lay awake for a long time listening to the drip-drip of the melting snow and icicles that hung from the sod roof.

It meant a release from the snowbound shackles of the long winter. Stockmen throughout the cow country were, no doubt, listening to the warm Chinook wind's welcome whine with mixed feelings. It meant salvation to their livestock that had survived the rigours of a hard winter. When the ground was laid bare they would ride forth to count their losses in the dead carcasses strewn across the rolling prairies. A dismal tally of the winter's toll.

For Brad and Chalk, lying there in their bunks in the log cabin, eyes staring into the darkness, it meant something else, and right now neither of them was ready to talk about it.

The cattle on both sides of the river had come through the

115

winter in good shape. Brad stood to make a big profit when the cattle were tallied over to the Bannings and Bob Rutledge. The cattle in other stray brands didn't count. Brad was only too glad to winter any cattle belonging to the smaller outfits free of charge. Brad would come out far ahead financially, and would be able to repay Shep and Chalk a good profit for the cattle they had bought to stock the KC ranch.

Brad Rutledge's mind wasn't on any such gainful thoughts. In a day or two the Banning BB outfit would be moving in on him, and the Block R were, no doubt, already on the way. Nothing short of a miracle could prevent the outbreak of that long-standing gun feud. And Brad didn't believe in such things as miracles.

But it was the news concerning George Banning that rankled. It had been a week or more since he had read the unwelcome news, and since then Brad had grown silent to the point of being sullen, almost surly. Chalk had finally quit trying to yank him out of his morbid state of mind, without knowing its cause.

Chalk laid it to Brad's unwillingness to get mixed up in a gun ruckus. He was unwilling to let himself believe that there was a streak of coward in Brad's make-up. But since reading Shep's letter, it seemed to Chalk that had marked the beginning of Brad's strange behaviour. It hurt Chalk because Brad refused to come out with whatever it was that was bothering him. He waited for Brad to break the dark silence, and the longer he waited the more uneasy and unbearable the black silence became. Chalk was beginning to sweat when he heard Brad's voice, low-toned, bitter.

'Remember this, Chalk . . . Joe Slocum's my bear meat.'

Chalk's big hand clamped over his mouth to blot out the glad cry of sheer relief. He'd been a damn fool ever to think that Brad had a yellow streak.

'You'll get him. Ol' Chalk will see to it, and I'll keep Ab Adams off your back while you get the job done,' said Chalk.

Chalk threw off his tarp-covered blankets and did a double shuffle in his bare feet, till he stubbed a big toe and let out a howl.

'How come you get bloodthirsty all of a sudden?' asked Chalk.

'Georgia's aiming to marry Joe Slocum,' Brad said flatly.
'How come you know that?'

'I read it in that newspaper I burned a week ago.'

Chalk stood over Brad's bunk, breathing heavily through
splayed nostrils. 'I got a mind to cut me a hickory stick and
beat some sense into you, Mistah Brad. Miss Georgia ain't
fixin' to marry nobody on earth but you. You got cabin fever.
Never seen me a worse case.'

It was too dark to see the white-toothed shine of Chalk's
grin, but Brad knew from the hidden chuckle in his deep-
toned voice that it was there.

Sleep was out of the question now and Chalk made a pot
of coffee. Brad lit a candle and they sat around listening to
the drip of the melting snow and the low, whispering whine
of the warm Chinook wind.

The hard-packed snow drifts had begun to soften at daybreak. The sun came up in a crimson blaze to tint the cloud-
less sky and touch the snow-covered broken badlands with a
pinkish glow.

At daybreak Brad and Chalk had scattered the hay and
chopped open the waterholes, and when the sun was two
hours high they shed their overcoats and worked in their
sweat-stained shirts.

There were a lot of cattle on the south side of the river
that would have to be crossed before the ice broke up. The
feed there was about played out and if the cattle were not
moved back on to the Block R and BB ranges before the ice
broke up a lot of the weaker cattle would die for lack of
feed, and those that survived could not be gathered until
fall. It all summed-up to the fact that unless the cattle were
shoved across the river on to summer range that would be
bare of snow inside a week, both outfits stood to lose a lot
of cattle.

From now on every hour counted, and it would require
every cowhand both outfits had to round up the cattle.

It was about noon when Brad and Chalk sighted the first
group of riders coming down the long ridge, with a remuda
and laden pack-mules. The going was slow and heavy for
the chuck wagon and bed wagon. There were enough horses in
the remuda to give each cowpuncher a string of ten head.

They would have to be well mounted to get the work done.

'That's the Banning outfit, Chalk,' Brad said grimly. 'I can make out Joe Slocum and one of the Banning brothers, riding ahead of the remuda, and that looks like Ab Adams with them.'

They agreed that there were some Block R horses mixed in with the BB remuda, and some Block R cowhands among the BB cowpunchers. They decided they must have pooled the two outfits. But there was no sign of Bob Rutledge and one of the Bannings was missing. And Shep was not among them.

Chalk slid his 30-30 carbine from his saddle scabbard and cradled it in his left arm. 'Looks like ol' Chalk is bound to make it a Winchester stand-off until Shep and Mistah Bob show up.' He walked into the big log barn and Brad followed him.

They swung from their saddles and put their saddled horses in separate stalls. Chalk dragged a wooden case of ammunition from under a hay-filled manger. He prised it open with his hands and tossed Brad a couple of cardboard boxes, each holding twenty-five 30-30 cartridges.

They stood there, just inside the half-opened barn door, and waited until Tracy Banning, flanked on either side by Joe Slocum and Ab Adams, reached the padlocked pole gate. Chalk levered a cartridge into the breech and fired a shot over their heads, so close that all three men ducked.

Brad stepped out in the open before Chalk could grab him and haul him back. He held his short-barrelled carbine in both hands, about waist high, and ready to shoot. He stood there, legs spread apart, hat slanted across his eyes, a growth of black whiskers making him look older than he was.

'Chalk can pick you off your saddles in no time flat, if any man makes a gun move,' Brad called out. 'No man comes inside my fence until Bob Rutledge and Will Sheppard show up.'

'Tell that quick-triggered Chalk not to go off half-cocked,' called Ab Adams. 'Shep will be along directly. He's travelling by cutter and the melting snow has slowed up his team.' Adams twisted half-around in his saddle to point with the ramrod of his gun, 'Yonder comes Shep down the slant.

118

Meanwhile, time's awastin'. We got our big round-up crew ready to cross the river. You're holding us up, Brad, and for no good reason.'

Chalk reached out and grabbed Brad and shoved him in behind the protection of the log wall.

'How come, Abilene, you throwed in with the Bannings?' Chalk called out the question.

'How come,' Ab Adams called back, 'that Brad Rutledge ain't man enough to ramrod his own outfit without you putting in your two-bits, you . . .?'

Chalk's carbine cut short the rest of it. His 30-30 bullet ripped a furrow through the high crown of Ab Adams' hat.

'Keep that big mouth of yours shut, Ab,' growled Tracy Banning. 'One drink of whisky and you get fighting drunk. I'm doing what talking there is to be done from now on.'

Tracy Banning called out to Brad Rutledge. 'Will Sheppard has the Banning certified cheque made out to you for feeding our cattle. It was his idea that the Block R and BB outfits pool their men to gather the cattle on the south side of the river. We're going to cross the river with the remuda and pack outfits and work from the south bank. If the Chinook lasts for thirty-six hours the river ice will break up. Every hour counts and you're holding up the work.'

'Where's my father?' Brad asked.

'I don't know and I don't give a damn where Bob Rutledge is. All I know is that my brother Taylor rode to town to meet him and Will Sheppard. Are you going to let this pool outfit through your gate, or do you want your fence cut?'

'You give the order to cut my fence and it'll be the last order you'll ever give. You'll have to wait at the gate until Shep shows up. Chalk will take care of any of you who has a different notion. I'll take care of Joe Slocum, personal.'

'Any time, young Rutledge,' called Joe Slocum, 'any place.'

'Shut up, Joe,' snapped Tracy Banning. 'Your quarrel can wait. So can the three of us till that drunken shyster Sheppard shows up. Dammit to hell, what's keeping Taylor?'

Joe Slocum pulled a bottle from his chaps pocket, pulled the cork and took a big drink and handed the bottle to Ab Adams.

Tracy Banning scowled blackly.

119

'Looks like you could put off getting drunk till we get these cattle rounded-up and crossed.'

'You forget it was your notion to fetch a keg of the stuff along, Uncle Tracy. I'm not getting drunk. Neither is Ab Adams. Not drunk enough, anyhow, to slow us down when the time comes.'

'You talk too much, Joe.' Tracy Banning jerked the bottle from Ab Adams' hand. 'Give me the cork, Joe. When you want a drink, ask me. I'll give you one if you need it. If you don't, you won't get it.'

Tracy Banning wiped the neck of the bottle on his short coonskin coat. He took what looked like a stiff drink before he shoved the bottle into the pocket of his chaps.

A few minutes later Shep drove up in a lightweight cutter. He took the situation in at a glance.

'You around, Brad?' he called. 'You and Chalk?'

'We're in the barn, Shep. We've been waiting for you.'

'Stay there in the barn,' Shep called back, 'till the last of this pack outfit crosses the river.' Then he spoke to Ab Adams and tossed him a key.

'Throw open the gate, Abilene. You and Joe Slocum take the outfit across. Tracy Banning stays here for the time being.'

'The hell you say!' Tracy Banning's face was livid.

'Better follow me, Banning.' Shep drove through the gate Ab Adams had swung open. Something in the tone of his voice, the look in his eye, forbade questioning.

Tracy Banning rode in behind Shep's cutter. Chalk swung the big barn doors open and Shep drove inside. Tracy Banning pulled up just outside the barn, his black brows pulled into a heavy scowl as he watched Chalk and Brad unhook the team and slip the harness off and put the two horses in a double stall.

Shep threw aside the buffalo laprobe and stepped out of the cutter, stretching his cold, stiffened joints. He had a leather-covered quart flask in one pocket of his coonskin coat, the ivory butt of a Colt six-shooter protruded from the other. The 30-30 carbine that had been across his lap he shoved into the scabbard strapped to the seat. He unscrewed the silver cap on the flask. The cap telescoped into a cup that held a man-sized drink. He filled it to the brim, gulped it down, and screwed the cap back on.

'I needed that,' Shep said quietly. 'I am the luckless bearer of sad and evil tidings, gentlemen.' Shep's right hand closed around the ivory handled six-shooter and his eyes fastened on Tracy Banning, who sat his saddle with his weight in one stirrup, his hand resting on the butt of his gun.

'Bob Rutledge and Taylor Banning,' said Shep, 'rode into a bushwhacker trap together. I was no more than a hundred yards behind them. There were four bushwhackers. When the gun echoes faded out, three of them were dead, the fourth gut-shot and dying. Two of them were tough hands hired by Abilene Adams, the other two rode BB horses. Before the gut-shot one died, he talked.' Shep's cold eyes were fixed on Tracy Banning.

'After I had patched up Bob Rutledge and Taylor Banning and got them loaded in the cutter, I went through the pockets of the four dead men. There was a new hundred dollar bill in each man's pocket.'

Shep's twisted grin lifted an eyebrow.

'What the hell you looking at me for?' Tracy Banning rasped.

'The dying man claimed those new bills came from Tracy Banning's wallet,' Shep said quietly.

'You damned lying shyster,' Tracy Banning bit each word off and spat them at Shep.

'I'm only repeating a man's dying words,' Shep said flatly. 'Taylor Banning and Bob Rutledge both heard what the man said before he died. I took Bob Rutledge and Taylor Banning to the Block R home ranch and sent to town for the doctor. They're both in bad shape.'

Tracy Banning, his black eyes glittering, straightened up in his saddle. He twisted half-around to stare at Joe Slocum and Ab Adams who were now following in the wake of the pack outfit. He stared at them for a long moment, his slivered black eyes murderous.

'This checks the bet to you, mister,' Shep said, as Tracy looked around.

Tracy opened his mouth as if about to say something, then his jaws closed with an audible snap.

121

'I'm not on any witness stand, Sheppard,' Tracy said flatly.

'Granted. But you're straddle of a dangerous fence. Take care that hide of yours doesn't get hung on that fence.'

'I'll look after my own hide.'

'You're welcome to put up your horse,' Shep spoke quietly. 'Stay here with us while Joe Slocum and Abilene and their cowpunchers gather the cattle and shove them across. I can speak for Brad and Chalk and myself when I tell you you will be safe here. But I won't guarantee your safety if you cross the river with that pack outfit.'

'I'm ramrodding that outfit. Joe Slocum and Ab Adams are taking my orders. I'd rather be gut-shot than spend any time in the blackleg company of a drunken shyster.' Tracy Banning whirled his horse and rode off at a long high lope to overtake Joe Slocum and Ab Adams, who saw him coming and pulled up to wait for him.

'Is my father hurt bad, Shep?' Brad burst forth with the question he had been holding back until Tracy Banning was out of earshot.

'We won't know until we get the doctor's report,' Shep told Brad. 'They were shot up pretty bad before they could open up on the bushwhackers.'

'If they were wounded badly,' asked Brad, 'who killed the bushwhackers?'

'Both men, badly wounded as they were, gave a good account of themselves. Shep took care of the kindling.'

'And Tracy Banning paid for the job,' Brad said bitterly.

'It was Tracy's money. He probably gave it to Joe Slocum to hire professional gun-slingers. Joe and Abilene used it to their own advantage. I gave Tracy Banning his choice. He turned it down. He has always backed every play Joe Slocum has made. Tracy is backing his play for Georgia. He had their wedding announcement printed in the newspaper. He and Taylor have had several bitter quarrels about that.' Shep's eyes puckered. 'Georgia sent her love, Brad.'

Brad's face flushed under the blackened scars left by the winter's frostbite.

'But this is going to tear it wide open, Shep. When it's all said and done, Tracy and Taylor Banning are blood brothers.

122

And Joe Slocum and Ab Adams paid Tracy's money to the bushwhackers to kill Taylor Banning and Bob Rutledge.'

'Tracy Banning has made his choice, Brad.' Shep's tone was final.

'Joe Slocum and Ab Adams will kill Tracy Banning if he chaws them out about the bushwhacking,' said Brad. 'It's like sending a man to his death.'

'Tracy Banning,' said Shep, 'has been looking out for his own tough hide for a long time, Brad. This is not the time to get chicken-hearted over a Banning. You're Bob Rutledge's son and he's expecting you to play his hand out.'

It was seldom that Shep used that tone, and his smile softened the rebuke of his words.

The short day ended in a crimson and orange streaked sunset that deepened into dark purple, and through the first black shadows of night they could see the big campfire on the south bank of the river and the black silhouettes of the men as they moved around the yellow blaze. The white canvas of the mess tent and bed tent showed, faint-shadowed against the snow.

Sounds carry far on such a night. And it sounded like the cowpunchers of both outfits were celebrating. Voices were too loud, the cussing a little too fervent, the occasional burst of laughter had a false ring.

Shep and Brad and Chalk stood outside the cabin in the shadows and listened to the blatant mingling of noises that had a drunken tone. Both the Block R and BB outfits had made an unwritten law. No booze or gambling at the home ranches or line camps or on the round-up. Whisky bred trouble. Whisky and gambling.

Chalk cocked his head sideways. 'Crap game . . . feller sho' talking to them dice, trying for an eight. Done made it. Listen to that man holler.'

But Shep and Brad were listening for something else. The sound of a shot. If, as Tracy Banning had told them, he was ramrodding the pool outfit, he was doing a sorry job of it according to the rules and regulations that govern a round-up camp.

'One shot,' said Shep, 'one gun ruckus.'

123

But that one shot never came. Finally the three men felt the chill of the night and went inside the cabin.

Chalk pulled on his big buffalo coat and overshoes and picked his saddle gun from the gun rack.

Shep looked up from the old newspaper he was reading. 'Whichaway, Chalk?' he asked.

'Chalk's on first guard,' said Brad. 'He'll call me when the moon gets high.'

'How about me. You can't deal Shep out.'

'You bed down, Shep. You look kinda peaked.'

'Never felt better in my life,' Shep protested.

'We've been doing this all winter,' Brad lied glibly. 'We got it down finer'n frog hair.'

Chalk went out the door and closed it on the argument.

They were three men against unknown odds, if it came to a show-down. But nobody said anything about it. Shep fixed himself a hot toddy before turning in.

'So long as Tracy Banning stays alive, Brad,' Shep spoke softly, 'he'll never let you marry Georgia. Even if you did marry the girl, with Tracy alive she would live in constant fear. It would be well to think that over before you make the mistake of feeling sorry for the man.' Shep shoved his ivory-handled six-shooter under his pillow and stretched out, fully clothed save for his fur cap and boots.

Somewhere around midnight, Chalk rapped on the barred door and Brad let him into the cabin that was in darkness save for the faint red glow of the stove where he had a pot of black coffee simmering.

'Midnight and all's well . . . I hope,' Shep's voice sounded.

'The racket over yonder has simmered down,' said Chalk. 'The fire's still blazing and it seems like Tracy Banning has locked himself in the cabin. Joe Slocum and Abilene are bedded down, side by side, in the bed tent. The fellers on night guard are dozing off their jags. Plumb peaceful like.'

'You been across the river, Chalk?' asked Brad.

'Had to keep moving,' said Chalk.

Brad finished his cup of black coffee and fastened the frogs of his short bearskin coat and buckled his overshoes. Even the warm Chinook wind had teeth in it after sundown. He moved into the shelter of the log barn and wriggled into the

124

butt of an old haystack that gave him a view of the cabin and cattle-shed.

Brad kept thinking over what Shep had said about Tracy Banning. He felt certain that Shep was planning to kill the man, unless Chalk beat him to it. In either case, they were killing a man so that Brad and Georgia might find happiness and peace in their marriage. It didn't seem right. It wasn't right at all. It was wrong as hell. You can't build anything that makes for happiness on a foundation of a thing like murder.

Even now, Tracy Banning was locked inside a cabin across the river because he was afraid somebody would shoot him in the back. Whatever else might be said against Tracy Banning, the man had guts, and the courage of his convictions, right or wrong. Tracy made no pretence of covering up his hatred for Brad Rutledge. He hated Brad for no other reason than that he had Rutledge blood.

Brad's narrowed eyes stared at the big bonfire across the river. A harsh, brittle sound choked his throat and he spat it out and the sound of it startled him because it was meant for a laugh.

Either quit like a damned coward, Brad told himself, and let a sick man like Shep and a giant Negro who knew the meaning of loyalty do his fighting for him. Slink off like a coyote with his tail between his legs. Or quit feeling sorry for himself and play his father's string out. If he had any Rutledge blood in him it was about time he showed it. Proved it to his wounded, maybe dying, father, and to Shep and Chalk, instead of hiding behind them, and above all, proved it to Tracy Banning whose money had hired the bushwhackers.

Either one way or the other. Ride away from it when things were shaping up for a showdown and let Shep and Chalk do the fighting, then come back when the shooting was over. When they'd killed Tracy Banning and Joe Slocum and Ab Adams, he'd come back and marry into the Banning clan and become one of the tribe. Shep and Chalk would clear the trail for the bridegroom. Why not swap his gun for a Bible and get himself a white mule and take up circuit riding and take his bride along and stake her to a hymn book? But

125

be careful not to let the white mule talk out of turn like it did in Chalk's song, because about the time he'd be in the middle of one of his sermons about peace on earth and good-will to all men, and if thine enemy smite you on one cheek, turn the other side of your face, the white mule would bray to the wide world how he was nothing but a fourflushing damned rank coward who ran away. Sure Shep and Chalk would do his fighting for him. They had been doing it for years. . . .

The shot that came from across the river sounded loud as a cannon.

'Roll out you drunken . . . !' Tracy Banning bellowed through the gun echoes of his shot in the air. 'Roll out!'

Brad could make him out now, standing against the fire-light, a six-shooter in his hand.

Men came piling out of the bed tent as the last echoes of Tracy's shot were flung back from the broken badlands.

When Chalk and Shep stepped out of the cabin into the moonlight, Brad headed for them, carrying his saddle carbine in the crook of his arm.

'Two o'clock in the morning,' Shep said flatly. 'Tracy Banning gets up early.'

They could hear the round-up cook calling the men to breakfast, and the jingle of horse-bells as the nighthawk hazed his horses into the corral.

They could hear Tracy Banning as his voice broke through the other sounds. 'Rattle your hocks, Joe. See to it that every BB cowhand earns his pay. That means you too, Adams. I want every damned BB and Block R cowhand back at the head of the breaks by daylight. I want a clean work. Pick up everything that can travel, but don't crowd them too hard. I want those cattle, every head of them, across the river by dark.'

Tracy Banning stood waiting for any kind of protest. When nobody spoke, he barked his further orders.

'Tie into the grub. I'm giving you ten minutes to eat. Then saddle-up and get the hell gone. I want those cattle here by sundown. Have at it.'

Somebody must have said something about needing a drink

126

of whisky. It got a rise out of Tracy Banning. They could hear his angry bellow plain across the river.

'You had more than your share last night, you hung-over . . . ! I got what's left in the keg in my cabin. I'll shoot the man that goes near it. You'll get your first drink at sun-down, not before. If there's any more bellyaching, now's the time to get it out of your systems.'

Tracy Banning, still gripping his gun, backed away from the glow of the firelight and was lost in the dark shadows beyond. Somewhere, hidden by the night, he watched his sullen crew of cowhands. Most of all he kept a wary eye on Joe Slocum and Abilene Adams.

'Tough as a boot,' said Chalk, paying Tracy Banning a reluctant compliment.

'Cold-nerved,' Shep added.

'He spoke like he was staying at camp.' Brad voiced his thoughts aloud.

Shep gave Brad a hard look.

'Whatever you have in mind, Brad,' Shep said bluntly, 'forget it. At least postpone it until the cattle are crossed.' He turned to Chalk. 'Think the job can be done in one day, Chalk?'

'Shore thing. Mistah Brad and me has been fetching them in from the head of the breaks. There's a double crew working, and all the cattle are in fair to middling shape.'

'Time's up!' Tracy Banning's harsh shout sounded. 'Catch your circle horses!'

Less than a quarter-hour later the circle riders were under way. Joe Slocum riding in the lead of the BB cowpunchers and Ab Adams leading circle for the Block R.

There was nobody left at camp but the cook and horse-wrangler and Tracy Banning.

Back in the badlands a wolf howled at the moon that was dropping down below a ragged skyline.

Brad and Shep and Chalk stood there for a while in silence, each with his own thoughts. Shep struck a match to look at his watch. It was three o'clock in the morning. There was no sense in going back to bed. Chalk cooked an early breakfast. Nobody felt like talking. They all felt the let down, and at the same time a tension knotted their bellies.

A little past sunrise Brad and Chalk had finished scattering the hay. There was no need to open the water holes. The warm wind had done that job.

On the south side of the river they could see Tracy Banning and the horse-wrangler scattering hay for the remuda.

The sun was about noon-high when Tracy Banning rode across the river. The melted snow and slush ice lay like a shimmering lake on the river ice, and Tracy Banning was riding up and down and back and forth to test the ice. Then he headed for the north bank.

Shep had tidied up the cabin and had gone to the barn where Brad and Chalk were puttering around. When Tracy Banning rode up to where they stood, he looked at them for a long moment before he broke the silence. His eyes were bloodshot, wicked, and his gloved hands rested on the saddle horn.

'I found out last night,' he said, 'who killed Crowe. It was Abilene Adams.'

Brad and Chalk looked at one another. Neither of them was ready to believe that flat statement without proof to back it up. Shep looked up at Tracy Banning and smiled thinly. Tracy was scowling blackly.

'You can take it or leave it,' Tracy said. 'I rode over to tell you. It clears young Rutledge and Chalk of having a hand in the killing.' Tracy Banning leaned forward a little and his grin was ugly. 'But that don't clear Bob Rutledge. Adams is working for the Block R and so was Crowe. Rutledge will have to prove in court that Crowe and Adams were not taking his orders.'

Shep's thin smile twisted. 'Whisky talk, Tracy. How many drinks have you had since two o'clock this morning?'

'Speak for yourself, Sheppard. I rode over here to clear young Rutledge and Chalk of a murder charge, not to pick a quarrel with a drunken shyster.'

'You came over here,' Shep said quietly, 'to clear Joe Slocum of murder.'

'Ab Adams killed Crowe in the cabin. Joe Slocum never laid a hand on the man. Don't try to pull one of your damned shyster tricks,' rasped Tracy Banning.

'Joe Slocum and a BB tough cowhand called Buck, who

128

drove the sled, watched the murder through the window,' said Shep. 'Buck was the BB bushwhacker that puked up his guts before he died, after shooting Bob Rutledge and Taylor Banning. Both the wounded men heard him tell it. On the strength of that confession I cleared Brad Rutledge and Chalk before I left town. The sheriff and his posse are on their way here to arrest Adams and Slocum.'

Tracy Banning spat a brown stream of chewing tobacco into the slush between Shep's feet.

'Cousin Joe Slocum,' continued Shep, 'is accessory to the crime of cold-blooded premeditated murder and therefore guilty of Crowe's murder along with Abilene Adams. Buck's dying confession will hang both men.'

'Dying men can lie, Sheppard.'

'This one didn't, Banning. Crowe and Buck were pardners.'

'You're busting a gut, shyster, trying to hang a murder charge on Joe Slocum.'

'It's about time, Banning, that you swallowed some of your pride and stayed on our side of the river. I think you are aware of the fact that Joe Slocum and Abilene Adams are planning some more killings, with your name heading their black list.'

'Since when, Sheppard, have you become so damned solicitous of the Bannings? If you think you're ingratiating young Rutledge into the Banning family, you're mistaken. So long as I'm alive there'll be no mixing of the Banning and Rutledge blood. You look after your own scurvy hides. I'll take care of mine!'

Tracy Banning's bloodshot black eyes glittered. He reined his horse and headed back across the river.

They watched him while he crossed the ice, covered now by several inches of water that left the ice underneath as smooth and slick as glass.

'That relieves one of us,' Shep said grimly, 'of an unpleasant task.'

Tracy Banning was riding a horse that was sharp-shod, and the sharp horseshoes bit into the slick ice.

"They'll never cross cattle on that slick ice,' said Brad, as he watched Banning's horse. 'Every cow-brute will split.'

Brad spoke the truth. Cattle on slick ice go down, their hind legs spreading, their cloven hoofs slick, slipping. Like a toe dancer doing the splits. And the spread injury is permanent if nobody is there to tail the fallen animal to its feet.

Tracy Banning was aware of it before he was half-way across. They could hear him shouting orders, calling to the only two men in camp.

'Hook the mules to the hayrack. Drag the thatched willow roof off the cowshed and load it. I'll tell you where to dump the load when you get the hayrack filled.'

'We might as well lend a hand, Chalk, from our side. There's plenty manure in the shed that's not frozen that we can take down to those sand-bars at the riffles,' said Brad.

The feud was laid aside for the time being, the cattle work coming first. Brad and Chalk each drove a team hooked to the bobsleds that held hayracks. Shep discarded his coat and grabbed a manure fork, and helped load the hayracks.

They made trip after trip, building a twenty foot wide dyke across the water-covered ice between the two sandbars. By mid-afternoon the wide dyke was completed. The two crews, working from either side, met, and drove their work teams and hayracks over it back and forth to pack it down. The dyke was packed solid.

Brad and Chalk and Tracy Banning had all worked side by side, without speaking, dripping with sweat and their clothes mud grimed and wet. The job was completed by the time they heard the bawling of cattle. Both outfits had thrown their drives together and were bringing them now in one big herd.

'That channel ice,' Brad was looking at Chalk but he spoke in a tone loud enough for Tracy Banning to hear, 'will be honeycombed by dark. They'll be lucky if they get the herd across before it caves in.'

'That's right, Mistah Brad,' said Chalk. 'If them cowhands stop for likker or grub, it'll be too damned bad.' Chalk clucked to his team as he headed for the barn. Brad followed with his team.

Tracy Banning gave them a mean look and whipped his leg-weary mules to a trot.

'Get the remuda corralled!' Tracy Banning bellowed at

130

the horse-wrangler. He bawled at the cook to unhook the mules as he headed for his saddled horse. 'Get your kyack boxes packed and the pack-saddles on your mules,' he told the cook. 'Directly the men change horses we're moving camp to the other side of the river. No man eats or gets a drop of liquor till these cattle are crossed and the outfit camped on yonder side!'

'Even a prideful Banning,' Chalk chuckled as he unharnessed his team, 'ain't too high-chinned to heed the advice flung at him by a Rutledge.'

Brad grinned through a smear of sweat and dirt that covered his black-whiskered face. He pulled the harness off his team.

Shep was inside the cabin cooking supper. Brad and Chalk wolfed their grub, washing it down with strong black, hot coffee. Then they saddled their horses.

CHAPTER XIX

TRACY BANNING, mounted on a fresh horse, was shouting orders at his men, telling Joe Slocum and Ab Adams to string the cattle out. Telling the drag men to drop back and quit crowding the cattle, and for the men riding the swing to thin out.

'When does a man eat around this chicken-crap outfit!' bawled a hungry cowhand.

'You'll eat on the other side!'

'How about a shot of booze, Tracy?'

'You'll locate the keg where the grub is,' snarled Tracy Banning. 'When these cattle are across the river.'

The pack-mules were loaded and shoved across ahead of the remuda. Then the remuda was crossed, the horse-wrangler and nighthawk stringing the horses behind the pack-mules.

Joe Slocum and Ab Adams, riding the point, strung the lead cattle in behind the horses. Tracy Banning sat his horse on the river bank, far enough back from the strung-out cattle so as not to interfere with their walk-bawl progress. The lead and swing cattle were all big native steers, gaunt but stout and strong enough, while the drags were mostly cows, some with late calves following. When a calf became separated from its mammy, they set up a bawling din, and through the din came the shouting, mostly ribald cursing, the griping of hungry-bellied and whisky-thirsty cravings. Some of it was rough hoorawing and joshing, but there was an undercurrent of something more sinister. It betrayed the tension of every man in both outfits. There was trouble coming, but the trouble could wait until after the cattle work was done.

From the barn where Brad and Chalk and Shep sat their horses, they watched the pack outfit and remuda and the lead steers crossing, ears cocked to catch the talk that was hollered back and forth.

'Them cowhands is shore sulled,' said Chalk. 'Shore got a cod down.'

But the cook had a fire built at the lower end of the pasture, along the creek, and once the hungry cowhands got a bellyfull of grub they would probably take a more cheerful and peaceful attitude, they agreed.

'No man wants to fight on a full belly,' Shep said.

'Don't gamble on it, Shep,' said Brad grimly. 'If they tap that whiskey keg before they eat, watch out for the fireworks. They'll be drunker'n seven hundred dollars on empty bellies, and they'll forget to eat.'

The lead steers had crossed and were scattered out to graze where the snow had melted away in great patches, leaving the tall, dry grass showing through the frozen ground. Half the swing cattle were now across.

Joe Slocum and Ab Adams had come across with the lead cattle. They were both hollering at the ten or dozen cowhands who had brought the cattle across. Shouting at them to cross back on the ice and help the drag men.

Nobody paid them any attention. The men were headed for camp and the whisky keg and hot grub, cussing back across their shoulders at both Slocum and Adams.

'To hell with you two damned straw bosses. The big dog

132

with the brass collar said the likker was on this side. If he lied, it will be to his sorrow.'

Tracy Banning had ridden out a way to test the ice. The loud voices of the cowhands had filtered through the bawling of the cattle and the cowman had managed to hear enough of the scattered words to get the general idea that both the BB and the Block R cowpunchers had mutinied. When he saw Joe Slocum and Ab Adams head back across the river without so much as a single cowpuncher following them he drew his own conclusions.

There were no more than a handful of cattle remaining on the south bank. Three or four cowhands were hollering and swinging doubled ropes to whip up the drags on to the dyke that was now a sodden pulpy mass, but it still fulfilled its purpose. So far there had only been a few weaker cattle that had split, and those had been promptly tailed up on to their feet and back on to solid footing.

Tracy Banning cast a long, hard look at Joe Slocum and Ab Adams as they headed towards him. There was something about the way they rode and their half-furtive actions that warned him. They were separating now, making a pretence at testing the melting ice when there was no longer need of it. They split up to fifty feet or more apart so they could come at him from almost opposite directions, and Tracy Banning could only keep his eye on one man. It was impossible to watch them both, and he knew that they were planning to kill him.

Tracy Banning had known it for some time. Since last night, as a matter of fact. When both of them were drunk and each trying to shift the burden of blame for Crowe's murder to the other. The argument had been framed for his benefit. They wound up their whisky talk by saying that they were no more than hired hands and that Tracy Banning's hundred-dollar bills were as guilty as they were of murder.

Tracy Banning had crossed the river that morning to lay his cards face up, but one look at Brad Rutledge had changed his mind, so deep-rooted was his heritage of hate for the Rutledge tribe. Hatred, bitter as gall in his veins, was too poisonous a thing to be purged overnight.

Too late now for him to ride in behind the drag men and

133

the cattle. There was a hundred yards of open clearing to cross and he would have to turn his back on one or the other man who had it made to kill him. This was it. He had better think fast if he hoped to live.

Neither Joe Slocum nor Ab Adams had pulled their carbines from their saddle scabbards. It looked as if they were going to wait until they got up within six-shooter range, spreading farther apart until they got him in the broad middle.

If Tracy Banning shot first and shot to kill, he could get Ab Adams. And without the backing of Adams, Joe Slocum would quit cold and try to talk himself out of it later by shifting the blame for everything on to the dead Ab Adams. Let Ab Adams come up within six-shooter range. Tracy Banning asked nothing more than that chance.

Tracy Banning packed one six-shooter in the holster strapped to his right leg. His second gun was in a shoulder holster under his armpit. He was watching Ab Adams, who was angling to cut him off from the dyke, the strung-out cattle and the few remaining riders there. From the tail of his eye he saw Joe Slocum riding in behind him. Joe had a yellow streak down his back, and Tracy was counting now on that weakness. If he had been a praying man, he would have said a prayer right then. But up till now the name of God was only part of his blasphemous profanity.

'Closer, you Abilene . . . ,' he gritted, 'just a little closer, you Block R . . . and you'll get your ticket to hell punched. Quit sashaying off, quit shying away from me like a spooky horse. Nothing to get boogered about, yet. There's no gun in my hand. But I'll give you cards and spades, you bushwhacking . . . , and beat you to that gun your hand's creeping towards. What you scared of, you double-crossing son?'

Brad touched his horse with the spurs.

'Come back, Brad. Where the hell do you think you're going?' Shep's voice sounded sharp.

'To lend a Banning a hand, Shep,' Brad called back as he lifted his horse to a lope, 'before he gets murdered.'

Brad rode across Tracy Banning's vision, his horse slowed down to a long trot.

'Who sold you chips in the game, young Rutledge,' Tracy

134

muttered. And he found the answer to his own question. Brad Rutledge was taking Joe Slocum off his back.

'Why you young Rutledge whelp . . . finally come out to take your own part . . . I never thought I'd see the day when I wished any Rutledge luck. Have at it, rooster,' Tracy called out.

It was like racers jockeying for place, for the inside rail, to shade the other man by that split-second it takes to win. The split-second that means life or death.

Only a few seconds more, a few seconds and they all four would be within six-shooter range.

Then it happened. Without warning. The honey-combed ice gave way. The dyke and the last of the cattle drags and two horsebackers sank in a tangled mass. The honeycombed ice tip-tilted in chunks and spread with a slow rolling, weaving and buckling. The crackling, rumbling, crashing noise of the mass of breaking ice drowned out the bawling of cattle and the startled yells of the trapped men as they went down into the icy water.

Tracy Banning was the nearest man to the dyke, the first of the four to feel the water-covered ice weave and buckle under him. His terrified horse lunged, and when his forefeet hit he went down as if he had landed in a death fall, somersaulting. Tracy's gun was in his hand as the horse lunged. He thumbed back the hammer and squeezed the trigger, his slivered eyes still fixed on Ab Adams. The .45 slug caught Ab in the belly. The gun in Ab Adams' hand exploded a split-second later, but missed its mark by inches as Tracy Banning was thrown clear of his horse.

Ab Adams' horse stood braced as the rubber ice heaved and broke under its weight. Ab Adams doubled-up as his horse went over backwards. Sheer instinct pulled his feet from the stirrups and he flung himself sideways and landed on a ragged fifteen feet of floating ice, his gun still gripped in his hand, his narrowed eyes searching the open water for a sign of Tracy Banning. Tracy's hat floated on the water. His horse was floundering, forefeet pawing the chunks of floating ice. Then Tracy's head bobbed up and he made a grab at his horse's tail. He made it and hung on.

Ab Adams' harsh rasping laugh turned Tracy Banning's

135

head. Ab's bullet hit the water alongside his face. Tracy pulled a lung-full of air before he ducked under. He was clawing now for the holstered gun. When he came up for air, his shot blended with one from Ab Adams' gun. Tracy Banning snarled through gritted teeth as he felt the heavy slug tear into his ribs and chest, just below the collarbone. He shot again at Ab's head. Ab lay belly down on a weaving chunk of ice, and returned the fire. Lying half-submerged in the icy water, his aim was bad, and Tracy's aim no better. Only when their gun hammers snapped on already exploded shells did they throw their guns away and both seriously wounded men tried desperately to save their lives. Self-preservation was their only aim now.

A short distance downstream was jagged rock and shallow water, where the ice was slowly piling up in the riffles. The cattle were floundered now, belly deep in water, and the two drag riders and their horses regained their slippery footing and made their way to the shore.

Tracy Banning's horse found the precarious footing, and with Tracy desperately holding on to the animal's tail the horse lunged up on solid ground, just as the ice chunk that held Ab Adams jammed into the jagged rocks and lodged there.

'Throw me a rope!' Ab Adams hollered. 'One of you men.'

Tracy Banning was on his feet now, staggering alongside his horse. With numbed hands he jerked the rope from his saddle. Standing there, legs spread, blood from his bullet-ripped lung trickling from behind his set teeth, he shook a loop in the wet rope and threw it. Ab Adams caught the loop and shoved his head through it. He was reaching one arm through the loop to slip it down under his shoulders when Tracy jerked it, throwing his whole weight behind the jerk, losing his balance and falling over backwards.

Ab Adams let out a choked cry of snarling terror as the rope jerked tight around his neck, sliding free of his raised arm.

Tracy Banning, both hands hanging on to the rope, was pulling himself to a sitting position. His teeth bared in a bloody froth he pulled Ab Adams off the slippery ice cake. Ab Adams' hands were gripping the rope that was slowly choking him, hauling himself, hand over hand, along the rope. He was on his feet now and belly-deep in water.

On dry land now, crawling on his knees, using both hands to haul himself towards Tracy Banning and keep the rope from tightening around his neck, he cursed Tracy Banning in a croaking voice.

When he was within a foot of Tracy Banning he let go the rope. He tried to free the wet rope from around his neck with one hand, while he shoved his other hand into his pocket and brought out a big stock-knife. Still jerking at the tight noose, Ab opened the blade with his teeth. He grinned wolfishly at Tracy Banning.

Tracy Banning took in the slack rope quickly until it was taut. So intent was Ab Adams on knifing his enemy he forgot to cut the rope. Tracy threw himself backwards to tighten the wet noose, jerking Ab over on top of him. They rolled over on the ground together, Ab slashing and stabbing savagely, Tracy jerking and twisting to tighten the already tight noose.

The two drag men, one a BB man and the other a Block R cowhand, stood there, shivering with cold, their staring eyes watching the death struggle, until Ab Adams' face purpled and blackened, his jaw slackening in death. Tracy Banning, bleeding from a score of deep knife rips and stabs, rolled clear, but was dead in a few minutes from loss of blood.

While out in the river, only fifty feet of weaving, rolling, rubber honeycombed ice separated Brad Rutledge and Joe Slocum.

They had watched the dyke give way and the cattle and riders go down, and Joe Slocum stared with terrified eyes at his Uncle Tracy and Ab Adams shooting it out.

Brad had his six-shooter in his hand. He tilted the gun and his thumb cocked it on the down swing.

'Fill your hand, Joe!' Brad shouted.

Joe Slocum twisted his head to stare at Brad Rutledge. 'Don't shoot!' he screamed, dropping his knotted bridle reins to lift both hands.

He still had both hands lifted when the buckling ice broke under his horse, throwing him off into the icy water, arms and legs widespread. Brad still had his gun in his hand when

137

the ice cracked and broke and he and his horse were plunged in the water. He let go his gun as he hit.

Chalk had ridden out when he saw the first ice break. The whites of his eyes rolled as he took it all in. He shoved the carbine into its saddle scabbard and without a wasted motion jerked at his rope strap. The fifty-foot rope was in his hand as he quit his horse. He was travelling at a run now, lifting his legs high, each long leg spashing water. The coiled rope in his left hand, he was shaking a loop with his right hand.

Chalk pulled up short as Brad and his horse went down. With an overhand throw, the loop sped out, and there was a prayer somewhere inside the black giant that made it a lucky loop. His white teeth bared as he made his catch. He took a few quick steps backwards, bracing his feet, and with a long heave he had Brad out of the cold water and on the ice. Standing there on the more solid ice he pulled the taut rawhide rope in hand over hand, snaking Brad across the water-covered ice with steady, swift pulls. When Brad was hauled close enough, Chalk lifted him on to his feet and freed the rope.

Joe Slocum, weighted down by his sodden clothes and boots and heavy cartridge belt and gun, was gripped in a drowning man's panic, his arms flailing the water, his cries for help shrill now as a woman's scream.

'Rope him, Chalk!' gasped Brad, half-drowned, waterlogged and swaying groggily. 'He's like me, he can't swim.'

Chalk moved away from Brad, out towards the end of the solid ice. He shook a small loop into the wet rope. For the fraction of a moment that Joe Slocum's head and one flailing arm showed, Chalk made his throw and jerked the rope quickly, as Joe Slocum went under.

Chalk let out a grunt as the rope went taut. 'Done caught me a devil fish,' Chalk muttered as he commenced hauling the man through the water, hand over hand. With a final heave he had Joe Slocum on the ice. Joe Slocum landed heavily, and skidded across the water-covered ice to land against Brad's braced legs.

'There's that worthless devil fish, Mistah Brad.'

Just then the ice buckled and broke underneath the black giant's weight.

Brad's sharp cry, a half-moan, was lost in the cracking of the ice. 'Chalk! Chalk!' Brad yelled.

Brad jerked the wet rope off the limp Joe Slocum and started across the ice, just as Chalk's head and shoulders came to the surface.

'Get back,' Mistah Brad,' Chalk yelled. 'Ol' Chalk's a water dog. Don't come near me while I busts this ol' Missouri river like it was a wading creek.'

The two horses Joe Slocum and Brad had been riding were headed down stream, towards the riffles and the rocks that showed. Chalk was trying to overtake the nearest horse. With half a dozen powerful overhand side strokes he closed the gap of open water and ice chunks to grasp the tail of Brad's horse. But Brad did not see it. He had turned on Joe Slocum.

Brad yanked Joe Slocum to his feet and shook him. 'If the best friend I have on earth drowns, it'll be your fault, and I'll kill you.'

Fear was still in the eyes of Joe Slocum, mingled with hate. Brad had hold of the front of his shirt and was sobbing, dry sobs that left his eyes hard and pain seared with grief and a terrible fury, while he slapped Joe Slocum across the face time after time.

Brad never saw Joe Slocum's right hand close over the butt of his gun and slide it cautiously from its holster. He kept his grip on the other man's shirt and kept slapping him until Joe Slocum's head rolled from side to side. Brad kept sobbing profanity. 'I killed Chalk . . . sent him out there . . . to save a damned thing like you . . . I drowned Chalk . . . you hear me. . . .'

Brad yanked Joe Slocum off balance and his own foot skidded out from under him. Joe Slocum's gun exploded as they both went down. Brad felt the thudding, burning force of the heavy bullet as it seared his ribs. As they went down Brad let go his hold on the shirt and gripped Joe Slocum's throat with both hands.

Shep was on all fours out on the ice, crawling towards the men who were locked. He saw the gun in Joe Slocum's hand and made a grab for his gun arm and missed. Joe Slocum clubbed Brad's head with the six-shooter and Brad felt the thud of it alongside his jaw and skull. Dizzied now, he put

139

all his ebbing strength into the throttling grip he still held on Joe's throat.

Joe Slocum shoved the barrel of his gun into Brad's belly and thumbed back the gun hammer, just as Shep grabbed it and twisted. A hoarse scream was torn from the throat of Joe Slocum as his trigger finger squeezed on the bullet that entered his belly. Brad heard the gun explosion. His senses were reeling and he kept fighting off the black dizziness that swept over him. Shep had to pry Brad's fingers loose from the throttling grip he still held on Joe Slocum. Then everything went black for Brad.

While downstream the two horses were scrambling out of the shallow water. Chalk, still hanging to the tail of Brad's horse, pulled himself up on to his feet. Shivering, his teeth chattering, blowing like a spent runner, he headed towards Brad and Shep, where Shep was pouring raw whisky down Brad's throat. Shep shoved the whisky flask into Chalk's hands. Chalk took a stiff drink and handed the flask back to Shep. He looked down at Joe Slocum, who was laying on his back, glazed eyes staring up at the sky. The water across his belly was a pinkish red.

Chalk rolled his eyes in the direction of the round-up camp below the cabin, where the BB and Block R cowhands stood in separate groups, watching, waiting for something to happen.

When Brad came alive and got to his feet and Chalk had taken another big shot of whisky to take away the chill, Shep said, 'With Joe Slocum and Ab Adams dead, there's nobody left to ramrod the outfits. What men were hired with Tracy Banning's hundred dollar bills, lacking their leadership, will be willing to keep it secret. With Tracy Banning dead, it's up to you, Brad, to handle the men. Chalk and I will go along to back your play.'

When they reached the pooled cowhands standing around in an uncertain silence, Shep did the talking.

'Brad Rutledge is ramrodding the Block R and BB outfits from now on. Any of you men feel like quitting?'

Nobody spoke. Shep smiled thinly. He told them about the bushwhacker trap Bob Rutledge and Taylor Banning had run into and about them being badly wounded. With Tracy

Banning and Joe Slocum dead, the BB men would be working for Georgia Banning, should Taylor Banning die. And if Bob Rutledge died, with Ab Adams already dead, Brad Rutledge would be running the Block R. He told them that Georgia Banning and Brad Rutledge were going to be married as soon as they could locate a parson, and that anyway they looked at it they'd be taking orders from Brad Rutledge from now on.

A big rawboned cowhand stepped forward and said: 'Us fellers been thinking it over. Nobody's quitting the BB or Block R outfits. We got more than a bellyfull of feuding and killing. You tell us what to do, Brad, and we'll tackle it.'

'Thanks, boys,' Brad said. 'I'm plenty grateful.' Brad told them to tie into the grub and when they got the wrinkles out of their bellies to scatter hay to the cattle, dividing the chores among themselves.

Brad and Chalk took care of their horses and then went to the cabin to change their wet clothes. After supper, they saddled fresh horses and, together with Shep, they headed for the Block R ranch.

They met the sheriff and his posse a few miles along the trail. They stopped long enough to tell the sheriff what had happened. The sheriff said he would attend to bringing in the dead for burial.

CHAPTER XX

IT was sunrise when Shep and Brad and Chalk reached the Rutledge home ranch. The country doctor opened the door before they reached the wide veranda. He stepped out on the porch. The look on his face told them the bad news even before he told them that Bob Rutledge and Taylor Banning could not live much longer.

'Georgia Banning saw you coming. She said to tell you first, then bring you in.'

141

The two grizzled cowmen lay propped up in beds on the opposite sides of the room. They had made the doctor give them the verdict and it was a question of who would die first. They were trying to out-tough each other, and hide the truth from Georgia Banning.

Georgia met Brad half-way and his arms went around her. Her lips trembled against his mouth as Brad kissed her. He held her close while Shep told the cowmen that Tracy Banning and Joe Slocum and Abilene Adams were all dead and how it had happened.

Brad Rutledge gripped his father's hand. There was no need for words between them now. Deep sorrow and forgiveness showed in Brad's eyes and it seemed to Brad that his father was glad the end was near. When Georgia came to stand beside Brad, Bob Rutledge took their hands and held them together in his big hands, and said. 'The Rutledge-Banning feud has ended. You two youngsters find happiness together.'

Brad looked over at Taylor Banning. He went over and took the dying man's outstretched hand.

'I don't need to hold you to any promise, Brad. I know you will take good care of Georgia. My only regret is that I won't be at your wedding. Your way is clear now to find the happiness you both deserve.'

Bob Rutledge said his farewell to Chalk, and Chalk gave the dying cowman his promise to look out for Brad and Georgia. Shep left the sick room and came back with the rawhide reata in his hand, and stood beside the bed of Bob Rutledge.

His left eyebrow quirked. 'Well, Robert, it didn't hang you, after all.' Shep laid the rope beside the dying cowman.

Bob Rutledge smiled. 'I want you to keep that rawhide reata, Shep, to remember me by. Chalk's right, you're the smartest damn lawyer ever born. You kept me from hanging.'

Chalk had gone outside to stand on the wide porch. Head bared, the sunlight slanting on his grizzled head, the giant Negro, face lifted to the sky, tears wetting his cheeks, sang his hymn to God, who created all men equal.

The sound of Chalk's deep-toned voice came into the room

142

with the warm wind and the sunlight, and the dying men and the others felt close to whatever lay beyond life. The eyes of the two cowmen closed in their last sleep when the song faded and was no more.

THE END

Walt Coburn was born in White Sulphur Springs, Montana Territory. He was once called "King of the Pulps" by Fred Gipson and promoted by Fiction House as "The Cowboy Author". He was the son of cattleman Robert Coburn, then owner of the Circle C ranch on Beaver Creek within sight of the Little Rockies. Coburn's family eventually moved to San Diego while still operating the Circle C. Robert Coburn used to commute between Montana and California by train and he would take his youngest son with him. When Coburn got drunk one night, he had an argument with his father that led to his leaving the family. In the course of his wanderings he entered Mexico and for a brief period actually became an enlisted man in the so-called "Gringo Battalion" of Pancho Villa's army.

Following his enlistment in the U.S. Army during the Great War, Coburn began writing Western short stories. For a year and a half he wrote and wrote before selling his first story to Bob Davis, editor of *Argosy-All Story*. Coburn married and moved to Tucson because his wife suffered from a respiratory condition. In a little adobe hut behind the main house Coburn practiced his art and for almost four decades he wrote approximately 600,000 words a year. Coburn's early fiction from his Golden Age—1924–1940—is his best, including his novels, *Mavericks* (1929) and *Barb Wire* (1931), as well as many short novels published only in magazines that now are being collected for the first time. In his Western stories, as Charles M. Russell and Eugene Manlove Rhodes, two men Coburn had known and admired in life, he captured the cow country and recreated it just as it was already passing from sight.